CAT SCRATCH KILLER

Christy Montgomery Michael

CAT SCRATCH KILLER

Christy Montgomery Michael

All Rights Reserved, 2018

Helm Publishing

ISBN 978-0-9723011-1-4

Library of Congress Control Number: 2018960986

Reader Reviews

From the first crime on its opening pages, hang onto your seat in this fast-paced look examining the emotions, anger and symbolic messages of rage and murder. Christy really has a great feel for crime stories and the words spoken between killer and victim. She'll carry you right through this frightening story and killer's mind.

Ralph Hipp
Anchor/Reporter WIBW-TV
Topeka, KS

It's a simple question: Where can a scarred young psychopath go to find true love these days? Or just maybe a narrow and fraught path to redemption? Murder on the Orient Express meets an Amtrak train gone off the rails in the snowy Rockies, as Christy Montgomery Michael takes us on a grisly yet at times tender tour of human emotions, pain and primal fear, right out of the streets and back alleys of St. Louis and set to a tune of the Motor City Madman. All aboard, and tickets please, for Cat Scratch Killer!

Dave Akerly,
WILS 1320 Talk Show Host
Lancing, MI

DEDICATION

I am dedicating this book to my darling daughter, Talina. She is a beautiful, young lady who inspires me every day. From a young age, she has motivated those around her to do the very best they can. She is giving, understanding, empathetic, encouraging, dedicated, supportive and loving. She is a true inspiration.

Acknowledgments

To Dianne Helm, CEO of Helm Publishing, my publisher: who has worked so diligently with me. She is not only my editor and publisher, but my friend as well. Her love for the written word; and helping this writer to find her voice, is what made this book a reality. Without her, this book wouldn't be found on bookshelves today.

To Mike Harrington: for the cover illustration of Cat Scratch Killer. You truly are professionally gifted and talented. This cover exceeds my expectations. It was a true pleasure and inspiration to work with you creating this concept design. The cover is the first thing people see when they look at the book and words cannot express my gratitude. Thank you so very much.

To Ralph Hipp: for his valued opinion on the story telling of this book. I have always admired your ability to tell the news to an audience with such warmth and professionalism. You make it easy for your viewers to invite you into their homes each time they watch. Thank you for sharing those traits and skills in your heartwarming review.

To Dave Akerly: for once again showing me that his talents continue to soar. Thank you for taking your valuable time to read this story and give a wonderful review. Your words remind me of the skills you have, in publicly giving your opinions as you do on your morning radio talk show at WILS 1320 in Lansing. As broadcasting colleagues in the past, I admire your ability to be diversified in television sports anchoring to morning talk show host. I can't even imagine what your next accomplishment will be.

To Dennis Michael: my husband, for all your financial, emotional support, patience and encouragement, you've been my Rock. I don't know what I'd do without you. Twenty-one years together and YOU are still the one. I love you with all my heart. Thank you for the wonderful photography on the cover of the book. Photos you have taken in the past, proved that you had great skilled in capturing the darkness and charm of my character, the Cat Scratch Killer.

To my Parents: I love you both more than you will ever know. I would like to thank you, for your financial and emotional support, constant love, encouragement and faith in this entire process.

To Vince Patton: a very good friend from WFAA-TV, who generously gave of himself and his time to help me research the terrain of the rugged Colorado Mountains.

To Craig Harper (Frisco) and John Miller (Fort Worth, TX.): who were co-workers at WFAA-TV, for giving me the strength and tools to succeed, during my years at the studio.

To WFAA-TV, Dallas, TX: for believing in me and giving me opportunities (1989-2000) that surpassed other television stations I worked at in the past.

To Zach Clark: thank you for helping create the haunting cover image of the character for the Cat Scratch Killer novel. Your ability to bring life to the Cat Scratch Killer in the imagination of my readers makes you the perfect Tran.

To Janie Bryan Loveless: your expertise in giving me Chapter 1 advice, and mentoring throughout to help with grammar was invaluable. Thank you.

To the Bill Clark Trio: for giving me beautiful music while I write (via CD). Bill gave me strength to believe in possibilities for success among our fellow high school classmates (alumni of 1983) and our local community.

To Sharlene: a California Zephyr sleeper car attendant, who gave me the most informative and beautiful train journey, providing me with important train facts and train schedules. This book would have been incomplete with you. Thank you.

To Shania Twain: in my opinion is an Inspiration to women through her biography and music, motivating women everywhere to make their dreams reality.

CAT SCRATCH KILLER

Cast of Characters

Trandon (Tran) – son of Jackie, street survivor

Jackie – Tran's abusive and sadistic mother

Darren – Jackie's first real boyfriend

Skinner – Jackie's drug dealer

Jordan – nightclub victim

Kristen – friend of Jordan

*Talina – nurse and Tran's love of his life, train passenger

Jasmine – nurse, and Talina's friend and roommate, train passenger

*Bobby – Jordan's husband, and train passenger

Brayden – Bobby's son and train passenger

*Zack – sporting goods salesman and train passenger

John Mitch – Businessman, and train passenger

Jezzy – model and train passenger

*Pete – Jezzy's bodyguard, and train passenger

Arthur – retired executive, and train passenger

Doris – wife of Arthur, and train passenger

*Dennis – train engineer

Daniel – waiter on train who takes charge after crash

Kristy – Tran's last victim

TABLE OF CONTENTS

Chapter 1 Escape   1

Chapter 2 Derailment   17

Chapter 3 The Assessment   37

Chapter 4 Cry Me Wolf   54

Chapter 5 Rescue and Survival   76

Chapter 6 New Beginnings   101

Chapter 7 Obsession   117

Chapter 8 The Warehouse   136

Chapter 9 The Last Kill   151

Cat Scratch Killer

Chapter 1 - Escape

Laughter filled the air as Jordan and Kristen walked out of the nightclub "Crystal Illusions," a fun Friday night hangout in downtown St. Louis, Missouri. It was their Friday payday ritual to go to Crystal Illusions after work. Jordan had been traveling for the past week so midnight was late enough. She seemed to be traveling with her job more in 1992.

The winter November air was cold. But little did they know that they were being watched. Kristen was parked right in front of the club, but Jordan had a short walk. A man in his late twenties watched as they said goodbye to each other.

"See you Monday," shouted Kristen.

"Sounds good," Jordan called back to her.

As Kristen drove off, the man called the Cat Scratch Killer crossed the street. He walked several steps behind Jordan, clutching a black bag. Since others entered and left the bar, no one noticed him following her.

The man watched Jordan's hair bounce back and forth as she walked. She picked up her stride to get to her car as she started to get nervous being alone in the dark. He sped up his pace, closing in on the distance between them.

Jordan reached for her keys in her purse. The Cat Scratch Killer approached her from behind. He dropped his black gym bag, grabbed her with one hand while covering her mouth with his other. Dragging her down the alley, he then pushed her against a brick wall. He was waiting to be sure no one had noticed. He gripped her neck tightly as he stared directly into her eyes. This always turned him on; seeing a woman's eyes as he killed her. He imagined they were his mother's eyes. Jordan's strength weakened but she continued to struggle by pushing and kicking. Silent screams caught in her throat as frantic tears fell when she realized she would never see her family again. Her husband and son meant everything to her. Thoughts raced through her mind. *How would her son grow up without her? How would her parents handle the loss of their only daughter?* She could feel her body go limp. Everything went completely black. Her body had given up the fight.

Tran released his hold on her throat, then he let go and stepped back. Jordan's lifeless body fell to the ground. He realized he left his black gym bag several steps behind. He quickly ran back about fifty feet to get the bag and bring it to Jordan's body. It was time to leave his trademark. Opening his black gym bag, he grabbed his Walkman, headphones and metal back scratcher. He listened to "Cat Scratch Fever" by Ted Nugent. He grabbed Jordan's limp body, rolling her onto her stomach. He ripped open her shirt, unhooked her bra and began leaving his mark, with the metal back scratcher, tearing through her beautiful, ivory skin, leaving bloody streaks down her back. His rage intensified with each stroke. Slowly reaching its peak, the song ended. He replaced everything in his bag, wiping the blood off the scratcher with Jordan's torn shirt. The killer turned her back over and stared at the beautiful, doll-like, blue eyes. Since he had no means of making a living, he often stole money from his victims. On this night, he got lucky. It was her payday, and he found almost $900 in her wallet. She normally would have deposited most of it in her bank, but she was saving money to visit her parents in California.

As he left the alley, a door opened, catching him off guard. A man came out and locked eyes with Tran. Both men were startled. Tran couldn't run fast enough. *There was a witness.* The police would be looking for him. This was his first killing in four days. It was time to move on, before police caught him. He'd always wanted to fly to Colorado or Utah, but the detectives might search the airport. He never liked riding the school bus, so taking the bus was out of the question.

Tran then decided to take the train, remembering when he was 12 and took a trip with his grandmother, Louise. Some of his best memories were spending time with her. When he was young, Tran lived with his mother, a prostitute hooked on crack and dying of AIDS. He remembered their old trailer, and the men she brought home. His grandmother was his escape from a depressing home. Every summer she took him to her home to Cape Coral, Florida.

Tran ran to the basement of an old, condemned building. Police frequently scanned the building for homeless people, but never checked the basement. He used stolen candles for lighting. He slept on a mattress that he found in a nearby dumpster. The only contents he owned were in the black gym bag which included a change of clothes, a photo of his grandmother, the metal back scratcher and a Walkman with headsets. He also had newspaper clippings of his killings.

*****

Tran's mother, Jackie, had always told him that he was a bastard. She didn't know who his father was.

He recalled being 8 years old, lying awake hearing his mother's screams while she played her trick. He wanted to see if she was ok, but knew he got in trouble, like when he'd walked in on her before. Tran didn't understand why his mother always brought home strange men, but at least there were a few groceries the next day. Most of her money was spent on crack.

He could never forgive his mother for the man she came home with on December 26th, 1977. She brought home her drug dealer. With no money for crack, she provided sex in exchange for crack to Skinner, her drug dealer.

As Tran lay in his bed, he saw Skinner's dark husky figure in the doorway. "Your turn boy!" he said in a rough, low voice.

"No! Go away! Mom, Mom, help me!" Tran screamed.

"Your mommy isn't going to help you, boy. She sent me in here. Your mommy needs something from me, so I'm going to get what I want from you." Skinner went to the end of the bed, snatched Tran's blanket, grabbed the ends of his cartoon pajama bottoms and jerked the pajamas off Tran. He tossed them to the floor and abruptly flipped Tran over onto his belly.

"Noooo! Mommy, help me!" he cried out, but his face was smashed into the mattress and muffled sounds came out instead.

"She's not going to get what she wants until I get what I want," Skinner said, striking the boy in the back of the head. Skinner climbed on top of Tran, whose eyes and heart filled with fear.

Suddenly, Tran screamed until he couldn't breathe, feeling the bed rocking back and forth as he stared at the picture of him and his grandmother on the nightstand. As if in a trance, Tran was transported to his grandmother's house, sitting on her porch swing, singing their favorite song. His arms, legs, voice, everything became useless. At some point, he stopped struggling, paralyzed by fear, feeling as though anything in the world would have been better than this. And there was nothing for him to do except wait.

When Skinner was finished with Tran, he fastened his pants and left the room without saying a word.

Moments later Tran sensed his mother was sitting at his side, holding his hand. "Tran, can you hear me? Snap out of it. It's over. You're ok. I'm sorry but this is the way it's going to be. Skinner is going to be your new friend. He'll be back, so you will just have to get used to it." She quickly left his room before he could respond to her heartless remarks.

The pain and trauma of seeing his blood on the sheets was too much. Tran thought he was dying. He tried to stand up but got dizzy. Once he felt steady, he took a step and realized blood was trickling down his legs. He went to the bathroom and turned the bathtub water on. As it warmed, he stepped into the tub of water, sat down and washed off the blood from his body. He began sobbing uncontrollably.

Why did mommy let this happen?

"I hate you, I hate you!" he cried, hitting the water with his fists.

Jackie heard him as she smoked her cigarette. She didn't care much about Tran. He was just a nuisance but he did provide a way to get her drugs.

After that night, Tran became a different person. Withdrawn and depressed, he was always in a daze. Skinner returned weekly, through Tran's 10th birthday. This was one of worst memories that haunted him throughout his adult life.

*****

When Tran awoke from this nightmare, he was covered in sweat. He needed to wash up so he went to the local gas station and used their bathroom. He was good about not going too long before cleaning up. He didn't like to look homeless. Like most homeless kids, he told himself that he would be rich some day with lots of classic cars in the driveway. If Tran wanted to go out during the day, he would stay in places where it was easy to blend in with the crowd. This week, he would stay in hiding.

Tran decided to stay in the abandoned building until taking the 7:55am train route to Chicago by way of the Texas Eagle. He would then go from Chicago to Salt Lake City on board the California Zephyr. This long trip would help avoid police activity around him. The local news broadcasted his killings, so it wouldn't be long before the witness in the alley would give police his description to the media. He would sleep on the coach to Chicago, and then get a sleeper car on the Zephyr.

Christy Montgomery Michael

The alley killing was not his first. Most of his killings were out of opportunity. He didn't plan them or put much thought into each killing. Whenever the urge hit him, he struck.

On an average day for Tran, he would usually stay in the warehouse throughout most of the day and at night. He would find other homeless friends to hang with. When he couldn't find anyone to hang with, he got lonely and angry about not having a normal life as a child. Then, he would be wondering the streets, looking for a victim. It wouldn't take long. Even though the city did nightly broadcasts about a serial murderer in the area, ladies could still be found partying at night.

Before he knew it, Friday had arrived, and it was time to buy his train ticket. Tran didn't live far from downtown, so he decided to walk to the train station. It was cool out since it was early morning in the fall. All he had was an old leather jacket. As he started walking to the train station, he began to pick up his pace to stay warm. He could tell it was going to be a cold winter.

He watched the traffic rush by him, since it was getting close to 7 o'clock in the morning. Daydreaming, his thoughts turned to cars. *It would be nice to have lots of money and afford any car I wanted. I would pick leather seats and a fancy interior. It would have to be royal blue, my favorite color. An SUV would be nice. Infinity cars are really nice, too.*

Cat Scratch Killer

He walked past a closed liquor store, thinking it would be great to have a beer. Tran convinced himself to stay sober, avoiding police at the train station. Noticing a little dog near the front of the liquor store, he wondered what type of dog it was. He was a cute little dog. Most serial killers torture small animals, but not Tran. His grandmother's collie always gave him lots of attention. "Hey, buddy," Tran said. "Who do you belong to? If I didn't have to leave town, I would take you with me." As he walked away, Tran put his focus back on leaving town.

At the train station, he bought the tickets needed for the long journey. Using Jordan's money, there was enough to get both tickets with a sleeper car. Tran had the habit of calling them cabins. He figured if he could stay in his cabin most of the trip, the less chance of someone recognizing him from the news.

He boarded the train quickly to avoid being seen by other passengers. He found his coach seat and sat down immediately. After taking off his jacket, he covered his face and chest so he could sleep the whole way to Chicago. There was something about the sound and feel of the tracks, rocking and humming in a peaceful way. The whole feel of riding the train was calming. It reminded him of the times he was on his way to visit his Grandma Louise in Florida. He could hear sounds of others getting settled as he started to dose off.

*****

Tran fell into a deep dream immediately. He came home to find his grandma in the kitchen cutting vegetables for a salad.

"Hi grandma, I'm gonna put my backpack in my room and I'll be back out in a minute."

Louise smiled as she watched her grandson walk to his bedroom.

Once in his room, Tran stood in front of the closet. Slowly he reached out to open the double doors. Relief washed over his face when he realized his grandmother hadn't found them. The bodies of 4 women he had strangled were posed all in a row, sitting upright, staring straight at him with their eyes wide open. The eyes on the girls were greyish and smoky looking. Tran kept them dressed as he wasn't interested in them sexually.

He knew there was a smell from them rotting but he realized that he couldn't smell them. This seemed very odd. *Did I kill the women after my grandmother died?*

Tran was petrified that his grandma might find out what was truly in his closet. He dreaded the day if she ever found out that evil part of him. Closing the closet doors, he started to walk out his bedroom.

At that moment, his grandmother approached his door. She was holding a shirt that she had cleaned and pressed earlier for him. "Hi sweetie, I'm just going to put these in your closet."

Louise walked past Tran towards his closet. Tran tried to stop her but he realized she already had her hands on the handles of the double doors. As she gripped the round white wood knobs, Tran tried in vain to reach out and stop her.

This part of the dream played in slow motion; his arms wouldn't extend to reach her. He tried to tell his arm to grab her but even though he was standing right next to her, she seemed several feet away. He had experienced this before in his dreams.

*****

At that moment, an announcement of the Chicago arrival blared on the intercom and awoke Tran. He couldn't believe almost 6 hours went by and he slept the whole time.

Tran didn't have much time to waste. He had a quick change over to the Zephyr that was scheduled to leave at 2pm. It had been snowing a lot in the Midwest, so there was an hour delay with his connecting train. This gave him a little bit more time to search for the sleeper car he would occupy on the way to Denver. He began looking for the perfect sleeper car on the California Zephyr as he walked alongside the train.

As he stepped up the metal stairs leading to the train's platform, a conductor looked right at him. "Good evening, Sir. May I see your ticket please?"

"Oh, yes. Right here," Tran answered. "I'm looking for sleeper car 4." He told the conductor he didn't want to be bothered by distractions because he had work to do. Tran found his cabin and got settled in. He sat on the bench seat that would later convert to his bed for the night and drew the curtains for privacy. It was very comfortable and Tran could still see outside through the window. He felt so alone, his heart was racing.

Tran stared out the window watching other people board the train. He observed a coffin sitting to the side, wondering if it was empty, or if a body was being transported.

There was a beautiful woman with two well-dressed men boarding the train. She looked familiar, but he wasn't sure where he had seen her before. He watched an older couple holding hands as they approached the train. They seemed very much in love. He didn't know they were celebrating their 50-year wedding anniversary. The man carried a pet crate in one hand. Inside was a beautiful brown Maine Coon cat. She looked like a lion with the fur around her neck.

As Tran looked to the left he saw two young women in their early twenties. He couldn't take his eyes off the girl with dishwater, blonde hair about four inches past her neck and softly curled inward on the sides. Her hair looked like she was ready for a photo shoot. Every strand of hair was in place. Her skin had a baby's glow that fueled Tran's sexual thoughts, which surprised him. The girls had actually boarded the train in St. Louis but Tran didn't know this because he had slept the entire trip to Chicago.

As she smiled at her friend, Tran felt his heart miss a beat. He had never felt like this before. He had always hated women because of the anger he had for his mother. Tran was eager to meet this mystery girl, but how would he meet her if he stayed in his cabin?

He noticed a boy about six years old and a young man that appeared to be his father. Tran watched how they responded to each other. He could tell they were close but they both seemed sad. The father repeatedly looked up to the clouds, while taking deep breathes. The older man stared at the casket being loaded onto the train. He appeared to be trying to hold back tears, stroking the boy's hair, as if to keep himself calm. Tran just kept observing them. *Who was in the casket that made them so sad?* At that moment Tran wished he'd had a father-type figure when he was growing up.

Suddenly, he noticed the cute girl he saw earlier with her friend again. They were passing by his sleeper room. He opened his curtain just a little to see them. *Could this mean she was staying in a sleeper?* Tran peered at them as they walked by and went to sleeper number 5 which was across and down the corridor from him. His blood raced as he thought there might be a chance to meet her.

Tran closed his eyes once again. He heard the conductor shout, "ALL ABOARD!" and then the train started moving.

Listening to the sound of the train's engine, he tried to think of a song to help him fall back to sleep. He started humming to a familiar song. It was almost 4pm.

*****

As his breathing got deeper he faded into sleep. Once again he had the same nightmare about an event in his life that actually happened. It began with his mother's sexual screaming when Tran entered his mother's bedroom. He could see Skinner on top of her rocking and moaning. Tran knew Skinner would be coming to his room next. He couldn't take it anymore.

Over to his right Skinner's pants were hanging on the chair. The drug dealer always carried a gun in his left pants pocket. Tran knelt down and crawled to the chair so as not to be seen. He put his hand in the left pocket and pulled out the gun. He stood up with rage and shouted out "You bastard!" and fired the first round into Skinner's back. Skinner fell forward onto Jackie. It only took one shot to rip through his body hitting his heart. Blood squirted out of Skinner's wound and Jackie screamed in terror as she rolled the dead body off her. She leapt out of the bed, and then stood trembling next to it. She looked at Tran with disbelief. "Tran, what are you doing?" she cried out.

"I hate you, I hate you mother!" Tran screamed while unloading another shot into his mother's belly.

Cat Scratch Killer

Looking down in shock, she put her right hand over the bullet entrance and cried, "I'm sorry Tran, I'm sorry!"

Tran shot another round into the left of her chest. The second bullet knocked her against the wall. She slowly slid down the wall until her bottom met the floor. Her breathing slowed down until the beating of her heart stopped. Tran knew she was dead. He dropped to his knees, sobbing. As his tears stopped, he was mesmerized by the empty soul of his mother's eyes. For the first time she looked beautiful to him. At this moment, he would always awaken from this dream.

*****

After killing his mother, and her drug dealer, Tran was relocated to live with his grandmother in Florida. He enjoyed sitting with Gramma Louise out on her enclosed patio in Cape Coral which looked over the river towards Fort Myers. Her house was located right at the corner where the canal began. He talked about his dreams while she talked about the past. The next three years with her were the best of his life before she died of heart failure. Afraid that the Department of Children and Family Services would put him in a foster home, he ran away. Tran was only twelve years old and now he was homeless. He hung out with a homeless crowd of kids in downtown Fort Myers. This is where he learned to fight, steal, and survive.

Christy Montgomery Michael

Before his grandmother's lawyer could tell him of her will which left him everything, Tran disappeared. He skipped out of town quickly to avoid going into the foster care system. Tran would never find out about his inheritance.

Chapter 2 - Derailment

Tran awoke to the conductor visiting each cabin to get dinner times. "Dinner time sign-up!" the train conductor called out as he knocked on Tran's door.

Tran opened and responded, "Yes?"

"I'm taking time reservations for dinner. I have 5:30pm and 7pm left, since 6pm is filled. I'm sorry." At first Tran didn't want to take a chance on being seen but he wanted to meet the young girl he saw earlier getting on the train. He described the young girl to the train conductor.

"That sounds like Ms. Talina. She signed up for 5:30pm," said the conductor.

"Ok, I'll take 5:30pm," Tran replied.

"Very good, sir."

The conductor closed Tran's door and knocked on the next one. "Dinner time sign-up," the conductor called out.

A young voice responded, "I'm ready to eat now!"

"Ok, I'll sign you and your dad up for 5:30pm," said the conductor.

"Thank you," said the father in a faint voice.

"No problem sir." And what is your name young man?" the conductor inquired.

"Brayden and my dad's name is Bobby," the boy blurted out.

"Well Brayden, I will see you at 5:30pm for dinner." The conductor smiled as he continued on to the next cabin.

*****

Tran was ready to get out of his cabin for a while. It was only 3:30pm but he was hungry and couldn't wait for dinner. He went to the snack bar on the lower level of a different train car. Satisfied with a getting a sandwich, chips and soda, Tran went to the upper level of the viewing car. It was beautiful to see all the scenery with all windows on both sides.

As he enjoyed getting out and eating, he noticed Talina and her friend watching a movie on the TV screens in the upper left corners of the viewing car. It was fun watching them laugh at the comedy.

By 4:30pm, Tran was ready to go back to his cabin. He wanted to relax a little before meeting Talina.

*****

Cat Scratch Killer

Before he knew, it was close to 5:30pm, and time to go to dinner. He decided to change his clothes to make a good impression for Ms. Talina. Finally, he was ready for dinner. He was dressed in dark blue jeans and a turquoise button-down shirt that he found tossed out in an alley bin. It was a little worn but still looked nice. The only attire he couldn't do anything about were his white tennis shoes with blue stripes which looked very worn and dirty.

Tran strolled from his cabin to the dining car. It was nice to be able to walk around. As he approached the dining car door, he could feel his heart pound faster. He was not used to socializing with strangers. With his right hand he pushed the door button in. The door slowly opened.

Tran took a few steps and immediately saw Talina with her friend sitting at a table. They were staring out the window. He knew this was the perfect chance to get to know her.

A nicely dressed waiter named Daniel walked up to Tran to seat him for dinner. "You must be Mr. Jacobs. I was told you had requested to sit at Ms. Talina's table."

"Oh, yes, Talina," Tran replied with relief.

"No problem Mr. Jacobs. Right this way," Daniel turned around and walked towards Talina and Jasmine.

As Tran walked towards their table, he noticed Bobby and Brayden talking. The father listened to his son so intensely that

Tran had to stop for a moment. Bobby looked up at Tran and smiled.

"Hello," Tran said as he continued to walk.

"Hi," Bobby responded.

Tran kept walking and could feel his heart pounding faster with a lump in his throat as he approached Talina's table. So many thoughts raced through his mind… Would he have the right things to say? Would he make a fool of himself? Would she figure out all the bad things he had done?

"Here you are." Daniel came to a table with two women and stopped. "Ms. Talina and Ms. Jasmine, this is Tran. He will be dining with you tonight."

"Hello," Talina burst out with a big smile.

"Hi," Tran replied, trying to make eye contact.

"This is Talina and my name is Jasmine. We just graduated from college," Jasmine stated, attempting to start a conversation.

"I'm Trandon. Most people call me Tran," he replied as he intentionally seated himself next to Jasmine, facing Talina at their booth.

"What would everyone like to drink?" asked Daniel as he placed menus on the table.

"Ladies first," said Tran.

"Why thank you, Tran. I think I will have cranberry juice," Talina replied.

"I would like iced tea with lemon, please," said Jasmine added.

"I will have a coke," Tran answered.

"Ok, I will be right back with your drinks and to take your orders," Daniel finished.

Tran stole secretive looks at Talina from the corner of his eyes while he glanced at the menu, trying to decide what to order.

"Well, I'm going to order the steak. I can't believe they have steak on a train," Talina remarked with excitement in her voice. Talina didn't go on many vacations while growing up. This was her first time on a train.

"That is a surprise. I love steak!" Tran blurted out. "We have a cabin so our meals are paid for. So let's go all out.

I'll get the steak, too," Jasmine said as she laid her menu down. She noticed Tran trying to look up at Talina but then quickly looking back down. His hands trembled slightly as he held his menu.

Jasmine noticed Tran's nervousness. She'd been through this before. Every time she was with Talina, guys got nervous and ended up having a crush on her.

Tran had a dark troubled look about him but when he smiled he could light up a room. He knew when he smiled, he was a charmer. He scrambled his brain trying to come up with a topic for conversation. "So what did you two major in?" he asked as he laid his menu down.

Talina responded, "Nursing."

"Wow, that's pretty hard work. I hear nurses do most of the work," Tran replied.

"Yes, but it's very rewarding knowing you've helped people," Talina said. "The money is not too bad and there are always nursing positions available," she added confidently.

You can help me any day Tran thought. An uncontrollable grin grew on his face.

"What are you smiling about?" Jasmine asked.

"Oh, nothing," Tran replied, annoyed by her question.

Daniel walked up to the table with the drinks. After placing the drinks on the table, he placed an order pad in his left hand and a pen in the right. He was dressed in a black suit slacks and white pressed button-down business shirt. His black shoes had a shine the Army would be proud of. His black bow tie made him look like a waiter in a fancy restaurant.

Daniel looked at Talina. "May I take your order?"

"I will have steak cooked medium-rare, baked potato with sour cream, salad with French dressing and chocolate cake," Talina replied.

Jasmine watched the waiter write down Talina's order. She waited until he made eye contact with her before telling him her order. "I'll have the steak, cooked medium as well, a baked potato, salad with Ranch and cheesecake for desert," Jasmine replied.

"And you sir?" Daniel asked Tran. Tran was too busy staring at Talina. He couldn't get over how cute she looked just ordering food.

"Sir, are you ready to order?" Daniel asked again.

"Oh, I'm sorry. Uh, steak sounds good, medium-rare, french fries, and what is the soup of the day?" Tran asked.

"Broccoli cheese soup," Daniel replied.

Talina sat straight up and burst out, "Oh, I love broccoli soup. Change my salad to the soup, please. Sorry Tran," Talina laughed.

Tran laughed with her, "That's alright." Then he finished ordering, "I'll have the soup and cheese cake for dessert."

"Anything else?" Daniel inquired.

"Nope, that will do it," replied Tran.

Talina observed Tran as he talked to the waiter. She sensed a mysterious side. His eyes looked sad. Like he wasn't really happy but wanted others to think he was. She noticed his dark hair parted on the right side and layered on the sides. His skin was fair but a little rough.

"Looks like it's been snowing a lot out here," Talina remarked.

The waiter smiled and responded, "Yeah, it's been snowing a few days now."

Talina looked back out through the window, repeating, "Wow, that's a lot."

As the waiter walked away, Tran could feel himself tense up again as he tried to think of what to say next.

Talina started a conversation, "I wonder how they keep the tracks cleared?"

Jasmine giggled, "That's the six-million-dollar question."

All three laughed shortly as they looked out the window.

"So where are you both from?" Tran asked while looking at Talina.

"Well, I'm originally from Plano, Texas and Jasmine grew up in Springfield, Missouri," Talina answered.

Tran watched as Talina licked her lips. It seemed like she did this off and on. Tran felt himself staring at her but couldn't speak. He was in a daze. He had never felt this way before which scared him.

Jasmine broke the small awkward silence, "So, where are you from Tran?"

"St. Louis, Missouri." Tran responded with a little shame in his voice. He quickly looked down. Tran knew he had to be truthful in case he wanted a future with Talina. This kind of information could catch up with him, should it fall into the wrong hands.

"You don't seem very proud of it," Jasmine noted as she reached for her iced tea.

"Not really. But I did live in Cape Coral and Fort Myers, Florida for a little while," Tran said as he smiled at Talina.

The waiter returned to the table with soups and a salad. He placed the soups in front of Talina and Tran, then the salad in front of Jasmine. The train made a sudden jolt. Daniel quickly grabbed a hold of the bench behind Tran. This happened often on the train. The staff was used to grounding themselves.

"I'll be back with some bread and crackers," Daniel stated.

"I am so hungry," Jasmine said as she jabbed her fork into the lettuce.

"So, are the two of you on vacation?" Tran asked as he stirred his soup.

"Yes, we decided we would reward ourselves and take a few days off as a graduation gift to ourselves," Talina responded.

"Oh, that's nice," Tran said as he began to take a spoonful of soup.

The waiter returned with bread in a basket and crackers in a crystal-like glass bowl.

"Is there anything else I can get you?" asked Daniel.

"No, I'm fine," answered Talina.

Jasmine shook her head side to side as she didn't want to talk with her mouth full.

Tran just smiled as he swallowed another bite.

Talina reached into the basket of bread sticks. "The breadsticks look so good."

"Your meals will be out in a moment," Daniel commented. Then, he turned and walked back to the kitchen.

Talina and Jasmine both looked out the window at the beautiful mountain view. It would be even better if it would stop snowing so they could see more scenery.

Tran was more interested in studying Talina's delicate profile. Her nose was perfect and round at the tip. The bridge of her nose was straight and smooth. Her skin glowed. Her long lashes curved upward like they were reaching for heaven. Her lips looked soft and pink. Her strawberry blonde hair laid perfectly feathered on the sides and the back just reaching the bottom of her neck. It had that 80's look.

"I really can't believe how beautiful it is out there," Tran remarked as the train passed by the lights of a small town in the distance.

Talina smiled, "I could live in these mountains forever. I would have a wolf as a pet."

Tran chuckled. He thought the sound of Talina's voice was stunning, as if she were singing a love song.

"I'm serious," Talina quickly retorted.

"Oh, ok," Tran said, under his breath not wanting to offend.

Daniel began to bring the meals out to their table. "Well, this is easy. Everyone likes steak," he commented, placing the steak, baked potato and chocolate cake in front of Talina. The train jolted again which made everyone's hands grab the table.

"Wow, does that happen much?" Talina asked voicing her concern.

"Sometimes. It just depends where we are. We don't get it much in this area but there is a lot of debris from the ongoing snow and winds. The ground is really soft," Daniel replied. He served Jasmine and Tran their meal. "Is there anything else I can get for you?" he asked.

"No, thank you," answered Talina.

"Could you bring me some steak sauce, please?" Jasmine asked.

"No problem. I will be right back," Daniel replied.

As they began to eat, Tran caught a whiff of a beautiful light sweet smell. Could it be a perfume? He began to take deeper breath to catch another whiff.

"What are you doing?" Jasmine asked Tran.

"That smell, something smells good," Tran responded.

"What does it smell like?" Jasmine asked.

"Like perfume," Tran answered as he reached for his cola.

"Oh, that's probably me," Talina said as she put her wrist to her nose. "I'm wearing Giorgio's Red." Talina responded.

"It smells really good," Tran said.

"Thanks!" Talina said as she smiled with a little blush. At that moment she realized that Tran might be attracted to her. They stared out the window and the view as they enjoyed their meal. It was nice to be quiet for a moment.

Daniel returned with the steak sauce. "I will be right back with refills on your drinks."

"Thank you," Tran responded.

"Just let me know if I can get you anything else," Daniel said, as he left to wait on another table.

Tran was enjoying the time with the new girl he just met but also wanted to get back to his cabin. He offered to join them again at lunch the next day at 11am. They all agreed to meet up.

Tran went back to his cabin where his bed was already made. He sat up to watch the train go through small towns during the night. He couldn't stop thinking about Talina. This gave him happy thoughts through the night. He finally fell asleep around 5am. He slept through breakfast and as the train went through Denver.

Tran awoke at 9:40am as the train was going through Fraser Winter Park, Colorado headed for Salt Lake City. He still planned on joining Jasmine and Talina for lunch at 11am in the dining car, so there was time to get cleaned up first.

As it got closer to lunch time, he started heading for the dining car. Talina and Jasmine were waiting for a table. Tran was relieved when Talina waved for him to join them as they were about to be seated. The girls sat down together so Tran sat across from them. They were at the same table as the night before. They couldn't help but laugh about that.

As they waited for their server, they looked outside at the falling snow.

"I can't believe it has been snowing so much. That's crazy," Talina commented.

"I know. There has to be more than a foot of snow out there." Trying to keep conversation going, he changed the subject, "So….do you two have jobs?"

"No, but we do have interviews when we get back," Talina answered.

"The school helped us set them up," Jasmine added. "Once we get into the work world, there won't be very much time for vacations."

Tran looked at the table across from them and noticed the couple who had a crate sitting on the table. Arthur and Doris looked like a cute older couple. He thought it kind of funny that they had the crate with them.

Behind Tran sat a model named Jezzy and the sporting goods salesman, Zack.

There were thirteen people in the dining car at this time. Most passengers ate earlier and had left.

Talina and Jasmine had the view of the kitchen area. Talina watched as the waiter prepared the food for other tables. The room was cool so Talina stood up to put her sweater on. It was a beautiful violet red color. The color brought out the pink in her cheeks.

Quick as lightning, Tran got up from his seat, "May I help you with that?" Thinking that if he acted like a complete gentleman, nobody would suspect he was actually the Cat Scratch Killer. His grandmother taught him how to have manners. He started to enjoy this side of himself. It just felt natural around Talina.

"Sure," Talina demurely answered, as he helped Talina with her sweater.

Jasmine peered out the window as they passed the Granby area. As she reached for her glass, ripples suddenly appeared in the water. Feeling un-nerved by that, she looked out the window again. Small trees looked like they were falling in one general area. "Oh, my God! I think there's snow sliding down the hill, towards us!" she shouted.

With the amount of snow that had fallen, an avalanche had started and it was headed right for the commuter train.

Talina and Tran quickly looked out the window. Others who heard Jasmine also looked out.

"Oh shit!" Tran blurted out. He started to feel rising levels of panic take hold of him.

The silverware and china started to vibrate and make an odd chaotic musical tune. Suddenly the train car jolted forward, forcing Tran and Talina to the floor. He landed hard on his right knee.

"Ohhh...my leg!" Tran cried out in pain, as he grabbed his knee.

Talina got up to a kneeling position and grasped hold of the back of the booth as the train started tilting in the opposite direction. The force of the snow overturned the railcars behind their dining car. Screaming filled the air as the dining car tilted back and forth.

Confusion took over. It was like watching a movie in slow motion. Loud squeaking emanated from the train cars rubbing on the tracks. People tried to get up and run. The screaming got louder and louder as terror struck. Another big jolt sent passengers flying backwards into the air.

A tear fell from Talina's left eye. She had never felt this kind of fear before. The dining car kept teetering back and forth as more snow and small trees rolled underneath it. Dinnerware was pitched everywhere. Breaking glass and heavy chinaware made the noise even louder. Plates laden with left over scraps of food on Tran's table dropped on top of him while he lay on the floor, writhing in pain.

Further on, other train cars were snapped off their couplings by the force of heavy snow and trees, creating more loud crashes, sending new waves of fear into people. Each time a connected train car would turn over, the dining car would take a strong jolt. Passengers, who tried to get back up, were violently tossed into overturned tables, or walls, landing in broken glassware and jagged pieces of china. The train car continued to shake uncontrollably. Talina looked out the window in time to see a large-sized pine tree coming down the hill straight towards them when it unexpectedly lodged beneath their dining car.

Jasmine watched one of the other waiters in the kitchen area being tossed around like a rag doll, helpless to do anything. He finally landed on the floor lifeless. With tears rolling down her cheeks, she looked back through the window. "There's snow and fallen trees everywhere," she said quietly, more to herself than anyone else.

Suddenly, their poor car endured the strongest jolt ever as the connection to the car ahead of them snapped, breaking the two apart.

Cat Scratch Killer

The squeaking of the train cars faded as mountainous snow piled onto the tracks. When the screaming finally settled down, some crying and soft moans of pain could be heard. Everyone looked around in shock, but no one moved. Even Daniel stumbled as he tried to get up with all the debris on the floor. They were not yet aware that theirs and the locomotive car were the only train cars mercifully left standing upright.

It appeared dark outside due to the weather conditions, and then the lights inside the train car went out. Before renewed panic set in, Daniel's calm voice made an announcement, "Everyone; its ok. Give me a minute while I make my way to the kitchen. I know we have some flashlights." The sound of crunching glass and dinnerware was heard as he slowly stepped through the fragments to enter the kitchen.

His shoe nudged the leg of the waiter who was still unconscious. "Jasmine can you come here for a moment? I need you to check him out. See if you can get a pulse." Daniel resumed his search in the upper cabinets as Jasmine found her way to the waiter lying on the kitchen floor.

"I have four flashlights here. I'll give you one and take the others to the rest of the group." He slowly made his way back out to the travelers.

She bent down to take his pulse, and noticed he was not breathing. "Talina, please come over here for a second." Jasmine

33

frantically called to her as she tried to feel for a pulse in different areas.

Talina left Tran and came to Jasmine's side. "I'm not getting a pulse," Jasmine told her in a low voice. Talina reached down and placed two fingers on the inside of his left wrist. "I'm not getting one either." She noticed the swollen knot on his head. "It looks like he hit his head pretty hard on the cabinet." Putting her head down to his chest to listen for a heartbeat, Talina pronounced sadly, "He's dead Jas." She reached for a clean table cloth lying on the counter to place it over the waiter's body to show respect. Overwhelmed, Talina looked up to the ceiling and fought back tears. Jasmine put her arms around Talina and tried to console her. Witnessing the scene with Jasmine and Talina, Tran felt helpless, wishing there was something he could do.

Daniel's strong voice broke the silence, "We have four flashlights." He repeated to the group. "We will only use them when needed. We also have some candles that I can set out but only a couple at a time. We don't want to start a fire. When we all get settled in and use the bathroom, we will not use emergency lights and candles until daylight. These will be in a common area so everyone will know where they are," he ended.

Passengers were starting to shiver from the cold. Not one person noticed a tree had crashed through a window in the first booth. Thank God there were no passengers sitting in that spot.

Talina returned to where Tran lay on the floor. "Tran, are you ok?" she asked looking down at him.

He loved the sound of concern in her voice. "I think I messed up my knee pretty bad. It really hurts," Tran muttered, gritting his teeth while holding his right knee tightly.

"Let me look at it Tran," as she helped him stand up.

Even though he was in pain, Tran put his arm around Talina's waist, feeling her close. This made him crave more attention from her. Nobody had ever shown him this kind of devotion before except his grandmother.

She sat him back in a seat, and reached for his leg. "Try to bend your knee," Talina suggested.

Tran bent his right knee slowly while whimpering out in pain. "Ouch, that really hurts."

"I'm not a doctor but you may have damaged your knee joint. Just to make sure, you should try to stay off your feet as much as possible. Try not to put too much pressure on it while walking until you can see a doctor."

"It really hurts," Tran replied.

"I'm sure it does," Talina agreed.

"We need to get off this train before something else happens," Jasmine boldly announced.

At that point, Daniel felt he needed to stand up. "Everyone? Can I have your attention for a moment? It's too dangerous out there to leave this car other than to go to the bathroom. We need to stay in here until we know the ground is stable outside."

Each person tried to process what had just happened. A renewed sense of fear permeated the air. Would it happen again? When would help come? Would they survive this terrifying ordeal?

Chapter 3 – The Assessment

John Mitch, a business man who owned a chain of advertising agencies with his brother, looked around to see if he could be of any help to anyone. He noticed Talina and Jasmine giving aide to others. Then, he could see Doris had her husband's head in her lap, crying over him.

Unsteady, John got up from the train car floor and stumbled over to them. There was so much rubble on the floor it was difficult to walk. He knelt down to ask Arthur, "Are you ok?"

Doris looked at him and tried to smile, "My husband hit his head on the table pretty hard." Blood was dripping down the right side of his forehead from a half inch cut. Swelling and redness had already started.

"Let me get someone to look at that. Ma'am, are you ok?" Doris studied John's eyes and paused for a moment, "Yes, I think I am." Then a look of alarm came over her face. "Oh, no! Our cat, where is our cat?"

She looked around and spotted the crate on its side under their table about five feet away.

"No, No! My baby!" she cried out. Doris gently moved Arthur's head from her lap, and then quickly crawled over broken glass and other plate fragments to the crate. She pulled the crate towards her and turned it upright. Opening the door, she could see her cat was visibly shaking. Trinity was facing backwards, so she reached in slowly and tried to pet her. But when Doris touched Trinity, her cat went crazy. The Maine Coon cat jumped, growled and hissed at her. Doris recoiled, "She's never done that before."

John followed Doris's path towards the crate and quickly shut the door. "She's in shock and scared. Just keep the door closed for now and talk to her to calm her down. When she starts to look friendly to you, check to see if she has any injuries. It's important to keep her in the crate until she is ready to come out. She will feel safer in there and hearing your voice will be soothing for her," John said as he tried to ease Doris fears.

He stood up and looked over at Jasmine. "You have medical skills. Can you help over here?"

Jasmine smiled, stood up and cautiously walked to them. She knew that if she fell, she might get cut from all the broken glass.

Daniel pulled a chair aside and carefully brushed off slivers of glass and plate shards. He sat down and thought through several scenarios for handling this situation. Until now, his disaster training had never been put to use. Daniel tried to think of ways to remain professional and be a leader for everyone. He looked around and saw the survivors, noticing their haggard expressions. It was essential for them to know he understood how they were feeling. Climbing on a table, he commanded their undivided attention, "Look, I know all of you are scared. So am I, but we need to remain calm. It may take a while before help arrives. It's still snowing out there and until the weather lets up, we need to take care of ourselves. So, let's work together and come up with survival skills to get through this."

Zack stood up. "He's right. I've had plenty of survival skill training. Our best course of action is to stay on the train because we don't know what wildlife is out there. Plus, it is warmer in here with our body heat. We need to be protected from the wind and cold. Daniel's right, it's still snowing out there. Another avalanche could happen." Zack was an extreme adventurist who had honed endurance skills that would help them as they waited to be rescued.

John looked at him with a look of fear, "Who's to say if more snow won't move down the mountain and demolish this car?"

Daniel countered John swiftly, "We can't think like that, now. I don't know how long it will take for help to come. If you need to go to the bathroom, don't walk too far. Stay near the tracks or you could get lost. Like Zack said, 'We don't know what wildlife is out there.' Take someone with when you go. Use the buddy system. We also should have plenty of food, but we still need to ration. The last thing we need is to run out of food and water."

The group realized they were going to need to make preparations for staying in the dining car, so they started by making themselves beds, using the table clothes, curtains and anything else they could find. They cleaned up most of the broken china and glass, food, silverware and other debris from the floor. Everyone tried to remain in good spirits, doing the best they could with so little light.

As Jasmine went to work cleaning the blood from Arthur's face, she realized that he needed stitches. She stood up and spotted Daniel. "Is there a first aid kit in here?" she asked him.

"Yes, I believe we have one in the cabinet above the sink." Daniel went to the sink and pulled down a small first aid kit which he opened to find everything needed to stitch deep wounds. Most first aid kits don't have needles and Lidocaine but since they worked in a kitchen, it was supplied for cuts and burns. Relieved, he took it over to Jasmine and she wasted no time getting Arthur patched up. Doris finally calmed down a little when she could see that her husband was going to be alright. Arthur wasn't talking much. He was exhausted and light headed but coherent enough to provide short answers to the questions Jasmine and Doris asked of him.

When the train derailed, the engine car stayed upright, while the baggage car, staff's dorm car and both sleeper cars broke apart and were swept down the hill. The Café/Lounge viewing car and three coach cars that were behind the dining car were also lost. The only cars left standing included the engine car and the dining car.

Suddenly, there was a knock. Everyone looked around in confusion. For a second, they thought they were being rescued. Daniel was closest to push open the door that faced the train engine. There was a man standing there. He recognized Dennis, one of the engineer from the train. As he opened the door, a sigh of relief came over the man's face.

"Oh, thank God," Dennis said. He came inside and Daniel updated him on the plans for the group. Aside from a few bruises and scrapes, he didn't seem to have any life threatening injuries. Daniel introduced him to the rest of the passengers, "Everyone, this is Dennis, the train's assistant engineer."

Dennis motioned Daniel aside to the corner. He had a very serious look on his face and at one point started to tear up. When the two men finished, Daniel made eye contact with John and told him he needed to talk to him.

"Dennis has informed me that the body of the main engineer is deceased and left in the engine car, to protect him from the environment until we are rescued."

"Is there anything we can do?

"Not really. We just need to make sure that no one goes into that car before help comes. The cold temperatures will help keep the body preserved for the coroner."

They agreed to relocate the deceased waiter as well to the engine car for protection and preservation. Daniel and Dennis moved the body of the waiter quickly in order to avoid creating more stress for the surviving passengers.

Jezzy, a young girl in her twenties, sat over in a booth near the kitchen. She had been having dinner with her body guard, Pete, when the avalanche occurred. He now tried to console her. She had minor cuts from flying glass. Small fragments were embedded in her face and arms. She was sure that her career as a model was over. Pete tried to convince her that all the cuts were very small and would not leave a scar. Tran vaguely remembered seeing her board the train with two men. He was not aware that the other gentleman stayed in the cabin to protect Jezzy's belongings.

Bobby was busy holding and rocking his son, Brayden. It was bad enough that Jordan's family lived in a small town in Utah and now this. As he comforted his son, he thought about the loss of his wife, Jordan. He was stunned that they had to face more tragedy in their lives. While he was grateful they were not hurt, he was concerned about the lasting effect this would have on his son. Brayden kept his face hidden in his father's shirt as he could not bear to look at the scene in front of them.

Talina looked over and noticed Bobby could use some help. She walked over to them and knelt down. "Is this your son?" she asked Bobby.

"Yes, his name is Brayden," Bobby replied.

At that moment, Brayden slowly lifted his head and turned to look at Talina. His face was blotchy from crying and teary-eyed. Talina felt sorry for him.

She smiled while speaking to him in a soft voice. "Brayden, we are going to do our best to get through this. The best thing is you and your dad are alright. Can you help me make a bed for you and your dad?" Talina asked.

At hearing her voice, Brayden began to cry, "I'm scared."

Bobby ran his fingers through Brayden's hair. He was trying to be strong for his son. "It's ok buddy. We are all scared."

Talina reached out to hold Brayden's right hand. "I'm a little scared too but now I just want to get through this the best I can. Sometimes, keeping yourself busy can help," Talina calmly stated.

Brayden pulled himself out of his dad's arms and squeezed Talina's hand. "Ok, I can help," Brayden replied.

As Talina stood up, she looked at Bobby. Bobby smiled and mouthed, "Thank you."

Talina smiled and took Brayden to help find materials to use for bedding.

By now, Tran had decided to make himself a bed under the table they had been sitting at. When he finished, he sat in the booth and watched Talina as she continued to help others. As hectic as this was, it was a nice distraction for him.

Jasmine took a break to see how Tran was doing. His knee was hurting but she tried to get him to elevate it. Tran told her he felt better when he rested. So she left him alone.

When Jasmine could see that Talina was helping the last person, she decided to make sleeping areas for her and Talina. It wasn't easy since most of the table clothes had been taken. She found several cloth napkins in a cabinet. She took all of them and fashioned them into half-beds, so they would be padded under the top parts of their bodies. There was nothing to use to cover up so when Talina finished helping other passengers, Jasmine explained to her that they would need to sleep close together to keep warm. She didn't know if this would be enough but that's all they could do.

A few hours had gone by while everyone was busy getting settled in. Dennis looked around at the remaining survivors. He was still in disbelief over the recent turn of events. He had been working for the railroad for over twenty years and this was the first time an avalanche had happened. He tried to imagine how the rescue would go. He hated the thought of the media frenzy that would follow. Then he thought of his wife. *She will be so worried when she heard the news.* He had two children who were grown and living in other cities. He desperately wanted to get word to his family that he was alright but when he left the locomotive engine car, all communications were cut off.

As the afternoon turned to evening Daniel stood up to make his last announcement for the night. "Ok, now we need to take turns going outside to use the bathroom before we all try to get some shut eye. Let's go in pairs of two to make it safer. Who wants to go first?" Daniel asked.

Brayden looked at his dad and stated he really needed to go to the bathroom. When Daniel heard him, he handed Bobby the flashlight and told them they could go ahead. Daniel reminded them not to go too far. As Bobby opened the door, cold air rushed in. It blew out one of the candles. Daniel picked it up and moved it further away from the door and relit it. Within a couple minutes, Brayden and Bobby were already coming back in. It was so cold that Brayden only wanted be outside long enough to pee. Bobby felt the same. It was also very difficult to walk in the thick, unsettled snowdrifts. They came back in shivering. Others paired up and quickly did the same.

As people settled in for the night, everyone's body heat began warming up the dining car. It was still pretty cold outside though. It wasn't long before all the lighting was out, and they laid in the dark, listening to the sounds outside. As the darkness lingered, the sounds in the woods got louder. In a nearby distance, a wolf started howling.

"Dad, what is that?" Brayden shouted as he grabbed onto his father.

"That would be a wolf. We're ok, Brayden. Don't be afraid. I'm right here," Bobby assured him, in a comforting voice.

"I miss Mom," Brayden said as he started to choke up with new fear.

"I know," Bobby answered as he tried to think of a way to tell his son that his mother had died.

"That wolf sounds nearby," Zack blurted out.

"Zack!" Bobby glared at Zack, hoping he would get the message not to talk about the wolves with his son listening.

Zack tried to cover his previous comment. "Sorry, we'll be fine..." His voice trailed off.

Bobby started thinking back to the night his wife was killed and didn't come home. He kept Brayden home from school the next morning. Brayden had been with Bobby ever since. That was how Bobby has been able to keep the news of his wife's death from Brayden. He was trying to figure out when to tell his son that his mother would never be coming home. He thought about the times they had together. Bobby and Brayden had a good life with Jordan. She was kind but spoke her mind, when needed. She had good sense. She often handled the bills since she was very organized. Jordan was raised to be family oriented. She made Saturday nights family night with a good meal and a board game. Brayden loved the closeness the three of them had. Jordan kept a very clean house. She made sure Brayden kept his room picked up. She told him that cleanliness showed that you cared. It was easy for him to keep his room clean since that's all he had ever known. Brayden loved his mother's cooking. Twice a week she would make a fancy meal. The other nights she would make something simple, like hot dogs or sloppy joes. He never knew that the meals were made to be healthy. Jordan would use turkey meat to replace hamburger in the sloppy joes. The hot dogs were turkey brats. He loved them. They were his favorite meal.

Bobby would cook occasionally to give Jordan a break. His idea of cooking was to barbeque on the weekends. His cooking was, as Jordan would put it, "Interesting."

Brayden enjoyed watching his parents help each other with cooking and other chores around the house. He could see that it was important to help keep a clean house and do what he could to make his parents happy. This would later help Brayden turn into a loving, responsible man.

*****

Unexpectedly, Trinity started to meow. Doris was glad she was making her normal sounds again. She suspected that Trinity needed to go potty but didn't know what to do.

Daniel turned his on flashlight. "Doris, do we need to make her a potty box?"

Doris was grateful that Daniel knew why Trinity was crying. "Oh, thank you. I think that's exactly what she needs," Doris replied. Daniel had made his bed in the kitchen, so he didn't have to go far. He got up and got a box from one of the cabinets. It was filled with small cereal boxes. He took the cereals from the box and put them on the counter. Then, he tore newspapers into strips and put them in the box. As he stepped over a couple lying in the aisle, he put the box under the table near Arthur. Arthur was already sleeping. He then went back to the kitchen and got a bowl of water and small bowl of cooked chicken he found in the refrigerator. He took it over to Doris. She took Trinity out of the crate and placed her in the newly made potty box. Trinity circled around in it a few times while kicking up the strips of paper. She then went to the bathroom which made Daniel and Doris relieved. The bowls were placed next to the box. Trinity hopped out of the box and immediately started eating the chicken. The cat loved meat, especially chicken. Daniel handed the flashlight to Doris, so she could keep an eye on Trinity. Daniel went back to his bed while Doris watched Trinity finish eating and drinking. She had left the crate door open and it didn't take long before Trinity went back in. She curled up in the back of the crate to go to sleep. Trinity felt safer in the crate. When Doris saw that Trinity had settled in, she lay back down and turned the flashlight off.

As Tran tried to go to sleep, he tried to imagine life with Talina. The thought of waking up with her by his side made the night seem easier. He imagined having a couple kids and playing with them in the back yard. Things that he really didn't get to do when he was a kid. He thought to himself how much fun it would be pushing them on the swings and spending every moment with Talina raising a family. The thought of being caught by the police never entered his mind. Not in this fantasy.

*****

This romantic thought didn't last long. The bad thoughts came back, faster than a speeding train. Tran reflected to when he was about eight years old. So many times, Tran was afraid to go home. He often went to a friend's house instead of going straight home after school. A day he would never forget was the day he went to CJ's house and stayed until late evening. It was a school night. As he walked into the trailer, he could hear his mother in her room with a man. He quickly went into his own room and closed the door. Tran put on his PJs and got into his bed. An hour later, his mother stormed into his room, screaming "Where have you been? You know you're not allowed to stay out late on a school night. Who do you think you are? Do you think you're something special? Well, let's get one thing straight. You are not special. You are nobody. You are a bastard that I have to put up with. You're lucky I don't toss you out into the street. Don't press your luck. I can kick you out at any time." As she walked out of his room, she slammed the door. Tran cried himself to sleep, as he often did.

This led Tran to think about his first kill. The first woman he killed when he was 17 years old. There was a young woman that lived across the street from one of his friends. She was a pretty Asian woman. After a month of living with his friend and watching the comings and goings of this woman, he got the urge for his first kill.

On weekends, he noticed she went out. Most Fridays she would head out around 8pm and stay out late. This helped give him a plan to catch her coming out of the house. He would stand behind a front porch post, facing the front door. She always parked her car in her carport. When she would leave, she always came out the front door. She would be all dressed up and wearing heels, but he was not interested in any sexual contact. He hated women too much for that. At times he could hear his mother's sexual groans and screams. The idea of sex turned him off because he always remembered this part. He was not interested in sex with anyone.

His anger and isolation from most women prevented him from getting an erection.

Two months from when he moved across the street from the woman he had been watching, he went through with his plan. He assembled a murder kit and put everything in his new black gym bag. This would be the bag he would use for all his future killings.

Most well-known serial killers have something they are known for. Since this was his first kill, he didn't have a trademark yet. He was a fan of Ted Nugent and his favorite song was Cat Scratch Fever. He packed his Walkman, headset and the Nugent tape in his bag.

On this night, he would fulfill his first fantasy of killing. He waited behind the post on her front porch. It was dark and the porch light was not on. It was a little before 8pm when the porch light came on. He knew at that moment, he could be seen by a neighbor. Immediately, the front door opened. As the Asian woman opened the door, Tran lunged towards her and gained entry by pushing her back inside the house.

He quickly slammed the front door to avoid neighbors from seeing what was happening. The victim's name was Taylor as he later found out from media news reports. He pushed her so quickly that she didn't have time to scream before Tran threw her to the floor and was on top of her. He had covered her mouth with his hands. She fought hard, but Tran used his weight to hold her down. Taylor was very petite, so she was easy to hold her down. He choked her immediately to keep her quiet and kill her.

He placed his hands around her throat. Her large, beautiful brown, glass-like eyes stared straight at him due to the grip he had on her throat. Tran was fascinated by the fact it reminded him of watching his mother's eyes when she died. Taylor was not able to fight with her hands because Tran was sitting on them, pinning her down. Tears started streaming down the sides of her face. His hands and arms started to get tired, but she was not dead yet. He could feel her get weaker but he had to keep his grip to finish the job. Finally, he could feel her go completely limp. Tran waited a couple minutes to be sure. He slid off her body, crawled towards the front door and sat with his back against it. Tran was out of breath and exhausted. After resting a few minutes, he grabbed his bag and took out his Walkman. He put the headset on and pushed the play button. As he listened to the song, Cat Scratch Fever, he stared at his victim's eyes. They were still open from the strangulation.

He didn't make any marks on her back this time. Those scratch marks showed up in the next killing, ultimately becoming his Cat Scratch Killer trademark. Still, this kill felt good and would be the first of many over the next several years. It would often bring comfort to him.

Cat Scratch Killer

*****

The survivors on the train could hear other minor strange noises that they were not able to identify. If they could get through the night, they could discuss further plans for survival the next morning. Getting through the night would not be easy. Most of the passengers lay awake through the night, thinking of the worst that could happen...another avalanche.

Chapter 4 – Cry Me Wolf

Morning came quickly. Brayden and Jezzy were still sleeping so the others went to the opposite side of the dining car. Those who were awake realized that this wasn't just a nightmare, it was real. As they discussed how they thought the rescue would go, Jasmine re-wrapped Tran's knee.

It was very quiet since everyone thought about how it could take several hours or days before rescue could get to them. This was the early 90's so most people didn't have cell phones. Jezzy had one but could not get a signal because of the weather, and the remote foothill location they were stranded in.

Zack finally stood up. "If we find other things to talk about, the time will go faster.

Tran didn't want to think about all the attention they would get with a rescue. Any rescue could put him in jail.

"Hey Bobby, do you have a wife?" Zack asked.

Cat Scratch Killer

Bobby looked over at Brayden who was still sleeping. He was only about ten feet away so Bobby kept his voice low in case his son woke up. "She was killed recently," Bobby answered.

"If you don't mind me asking, how did she die?" Doris asked with concern.

"She was attacked. Someone killed her in an alley as she was coming out of a nightclub with a friend," Bobby said as he began to tear up.

At that moment Tran sat up straight and shot a stare at Bobby.

"Oh, I'm so sorry Bobby," Doris consoled.

"Wait, isn't she the woman who was on the news the other night? Something about the Alley Cat Killer," Zack exclaimed. "Most of the killings were in alleys. Now the press calls the person "Cat Scratch Killer" from the trademark left on the victims' backs."

Tran listened to Bobby's story, knowing this was the same woman he had just killed the other night. He found it profound to hear how people described him.

Bobby continued his explanation of what happened, "Yeah, her name was Jordan," He reminisced. "She was a wonderful wife. She always made sure I was happy. She was also a wonderful mother to Brayden."

Tran listened as Bobby described Jordan. He started to question why he had killed such a good person. In the past, that was what made killing women easy for him, not knowing the victim.

Tran looked at Talina. "I'm going to go out and relieve myself. I'll be right back."

Talina joked, "OK, don't get lost! Are you sure you don't need someone to come with you?"

"No, I'll be fine."

Tran had to get away from the conversation about Jordan. As he opened the door, a rush of cold air came in. He didn't want anyone to go with him. It had stopped snowing and Tran took his time. He decided to look around after he went to the bathroom. On one side of the train, the hill went upward. On the other side, the hill went downward. As he saw the train cars below, a profound thought struck him. The cars looked like toys left in the snow. This scene didn't seem real to him. Oftentimes, Tran disconnected from reality, like when he was hunting for victims. He quickly went back into the dining car to tell the others. In seconds, they were all outside looking down the hill, in agreement that those were the remaining parts of the train. Most of them were on their sides. They discussed going down to see if there were any survivors until they admitted that it would be too dangerous. It was decided to stay where they were until help could arrive. All thought they were lucky to survive such a terrible tragedy, yet still unaware there was a serial killer among them. When the group returned to the dining car, Brayden and Jezzy were awake.

As they tried to get warm again, the conversation switched to Talina and Jasmine becoming new nurses. "I thought you two had been treating patients for a while, the way you were taking care of us last night," Arthur said.

"Thanks," Talina smiled. "It feels good to help."

The stress of the tragedy lingered, leaving everyone exhausted.

Tran went over to a booth away from everyone. A feeling came over him that he was very familiar with. Anger and sadness changed his whole demeanor. This happened often. Just like someone flipping a switch. He sat and just stared out the window.

He was thinking of good days with his Grandma Louise. He remembered the many trips to the post office he enjoyed. His grandmother had an assigned mailbox at the post office. Tran loved running in and getting the mail from her box. He always hoped for a letter from his mother. Even though Jackie was abusive, he still had faith that she would get off booze and drugs. He often hoped she would start appreciating him and start loving him. She only wrote him twice. That was just enough to keep him hoping for more. As quick as this good memory came, a bad memory followed. Jackie often had memory loss due to her drug use and drinking.

Christy Montgomery Michael

One night when Tran was five years old, he was awakened by his mother pulling him out of his bed and screaming at him. She was so angry. She thought he had stolen money out of her purse. She didn't remember that she used the money to buy booze the day before. As she dragged Tran to the kitchen, she continued screaming at him. "You think you can steal from me and get away with it? I'll teach you to never steal from me again!" she screamed as loud as she could. Tran cried and tried to convince his mother that he didn't touch her purse or her money. "Mommy, mommy, I didn't do it. I didn't do it, please..." he begged. It didn't matter. She was crazy with anger. She dragged him over to the gas stove and lit one of the burners. Tran didn't know what she was going to do but he knew she was going to hurt him badly, like she always did.

Suddenly, she got quiet. She looked down at Tran, then grabbed his left hand. She slowly pulled his hand over the hot burner. Tran screamed like he had never screamed before. He could barely breathe. He could feel the intense pain as it radiated throughout his entire body. Urine streamed down his legs as he saturated his underwear. His little body began to quiver. His eyes rolled back until his head tilted back as well and he collapsed to the floor in a heap. Tran had passed out from the pain and shock.

Cat Scratch Killer

Lying on the cold hard floor, Tran finally regained consciousness. He recognized the ceiling in their kitchen. His eyes started to come into focus. Then, he looked to his left and noticed his mom from a distance. Jackie was sitting on the couch, smoking a cigarette and watching TV. Tran was confused. He had never passed out before. This was his first but not his last. He began to rock his body back and forth as he had pulled his body into a fetal position, lying towards his left as he kept his eyes on his mother. He continued to rock himself while cradling his burned hand. After a few minutes, he stopped and anger quietly boiled inside of him.

He got up and slowly walked to the refrigerator. He pulled a chair as best he could up to the freezer door, got on and opened it to get an ice cube. Then he took the dishrag off the counter and wrapped it around the ice cube. As he put the ice on his hand, there was some relief, but after a few minutes, it caused more pain. Tran had second degree burns. If she had held his hand over the burner a few seconds longer, it would have been third degree. He learned that ice could help a burn when his grandmother burned herself while cooking.

Grandma Louise would always put ice in a sealed plastic bag and wrap a towel around it. She said this makes the skin cool, not cold. Tran walked back to his room and closed his door quietly. He climbed back into his bed and cried the rest of the night. He didn't get any sleep, due to the excruciating pain.

The next morning, Tran got up and went to the bus stop without seeing his mother. She was still passed out in her room. Blisters had formed on his hand. When his teacher questioned him about his hand, he said he burned it on the stove burner when his mother wasn't home. He claimed he didn't know the burner was left on. Thinking this would be a good lie because he knew that if he told the truth, things would be worse for him at home. He didn't realize that Jackie was contacted by the school and questioned about why he was left alone. By the time Tran got home, Jackie was furious. She beat him with a dog leash until his legs bled. She made him wear long pants until the wounds healed. There were some scars but people thought he got them like most boys, playing rough outside. This particular trauma would add terrible lasting mental effects.

*****

Usually, Tran's triggers to kill women originated from his nightmares about Jackie, or other women who confronted him. The rage inside would fester until he found a victim to kill. A past experience was when he was accused of shoplifting. A woman employee at the grocery store suspected him of stealing food and followed him around the store. He did have an item tucked into his shirt but was able to drop it into the meat case while leaning over without her seeing. Then he took a few items to the checkout and paid cash. When he started to go through the front doors security stopped him. The woman told the security guard he had stolen merchandise under his shirt. Tran denied it and was body searched in front of other customers. When nothing was found, they had to let him go. He was humiliated and grew very angry over the next several hours. The following night he killed a woman coming out of a gym. Women who worked out after dark, usually walked to their cars alone.

*****

As the day went by for the survivors on the train, Tran felt the urge to kill, not because a woman confronted him, but because Jasmine got too much attention from Talina. He seemed a little withdrawn throughout the day. Others figured it was his way of dealing with the situation they were surrounded with. He started watching Talina and getting jealous of Jasmine being with her all the time. It didn't take long for him to hate Jasmine. Everyone sat around most of the day, talking about how the rescue would go. Then, they tried to find things to do to make the time go by. Daniel let everyone use the back of the order pads as scrap paper. They played different games on paper at first, like Hang Man and Tic Tac Toe. After they had been up a couple hours, they looked for food in the kitchen. Daniel reminded them to not eat too much so the food would last. Once again, he encouraged them to eat the food in the refrigerator first. Because it was cold inside and outside of the dining car, the food was still good. When everyone got enough to eat, Jezzy talked most of them into playing charades. It was the first time they could laugh. Doris, Arthur, Daniel and Brayden just watched as the others played. Tran was alone by himself off from the group. Everyone seemed to enjoy the moment. When the game was over, reality set in again. The mood went somber again as their thoughts returned to the present situation.

Jasmine looked at Talina, "I need to go to the bathroom. Feel like going out with me?" Jasmine asked.

"Sure, let's go," Talina replied.

As they went outside, they notice it wasn't as cold as the night before. It was still cold but they didn't have to hurry so fast to get back in.

When they returned, they found Doris quietly crying. Both Talina and Jasmine sat down to talk to her. "Doris, what's wrong?" Jasmine asked.

Doris looked up, "Arthur doesn't have his heart medication."

Since Talina took an extra cardiology course in nursing school she asked, "Do you know what he was taking?"

Doris looked at Arthur as he was taking a nap. "No. It was a long name. His meds were in our cabin near the back of the train."

Talina looked down for a moment to think. "Do you know what problem he has with his heart?"

Doris smiled because she knew the answer. "Yes. He has high blood pressure. Two years ago he had a heart attack and got three stents in his heart. He also has high cholesterol." she added.

Talina smiled, "You did really good. That gives us enough to work with. It's good that he's resting. He should stay sitting or lying down unless he needs to go to the bathroom. Have Daniel go with you when the two of you go outside in case he needs help walking around. It's good for him to get out once in a while for fresh air and keep the blood circulating in his legs. When he eats, we need to make sure he is on a low cholesterol diet. There was some aspirin in the first aid kit. He should take one a day. It acts as a blood thinner so he doesn't get blood clots, especially where the doctors inserted the stents. Arthur's head injury seems to have stopped bleeding so this should be ok, but we will keep an eye on it just make sure. Just ask us what foods are safe for him to eat. If he has any symptoms, let us know. But again, I am not a doctor. You know your husband best. Let's work with that," Talina explained.

Doris felt comforted that Talina and Jasmine had some medical experience. As she wiped away her tears, a smile grew on her face.

Jasmine and Talina looked at each other and smiled. Without saying words, they both knew that this is what all their hard training and hours of studying were all about.

Jezzy saw Pete looking out the window as he sighed, "Oh, no!" Her eyes widened as she realized what he was looking at. Crestfallen, she lamented, "I can't believe it. More snow!"

John looked out his window, "Its ok for now. It's just very light snow."

Daniel could feel the tension rising in the room. He stood up with an idea. "Look, it's almost 6 o'clock. Let's start working on dinner. If we all work together, we can fix a nice meal for all of us. Let me see what we can put together. Let's focus on that and getting to know each other more, instead of this terrible event that we can't control," he stated with enthusiasm.

Zack smiled, "Good idea. I'll come help you. I'm known to be a cook."

Pete stood up. "Hold on. I'm the best cook in the room," he said with a huge smile on his face.

Everyone just laughed. Three guys were going to cook a meal that would not be forgotten. Zack found what was left of the cooked chicken. It was only about ¼ of a cup but he took it to Doris to give to her cat.

Bobby and John went outside to see if they could gather wood to start a fire that could be used for cooking. Even though the wood was wet, they were able to use sharp kitchen knives to strip off the outside of the wood from each piece of tree they found. They gathered small trees that fell down during the avalanche, including the tree that came through the window the night before. Once they had enough wood, they started a fire about thirty feet from the dining car.

As the fire continued to get hot, Zack and Daniel came out with all the steaks they could find. Pete stayed in the kitchen to make yummy side dishes from items in the refrigerator. Zack quickly built a stand to hold one of the racks he got from the oven. "Why are some of the steaks darker?" John asked.

Zack had a big grin on his face. Pete, our Master Chef, made a really good marinade sauce for a few of the steaks."

"Why are there so many steaks?" Bobby inquired.

Daniel knew that question would be asked and was ready for an answer. "We need to cook all the steaks before they spoil. They last longer if they are cooked. Once they are cooked, steaks are good to eat even cold."

As they finished cooking the meat, Pete came out with two cooking dishes. He had made a corn casserole and green beans with mushrooms.

"Wow, you weren't kidding about being a chef. Is that a side job?" Zack asked.

Pete was proud of his part in helping with the meal. "No. I used to do most of the cooking for me and my wife when we were married. I just enjoy cooking," Pete answered.

"Wait! I have a surprise," Daniel said with excitement. He ran back in and a couple minutes later, he came running out with four bottles of beer in his hands. "Who wants a beer?" he asked with a grin.

"Oh, cool," Bobby said as he reached out his right hand. They each took a beer that Daniel had opened while he was inside. Pete only took a couple sips as he was not much of a drinker. As John, Daniel and Pete took the cooked food inside, Zack put out the fire by dumping snow on it. When he finished, he was freezing cold and rushed inside. His hands felt like ice. It was warmer inside.

The girls had set the tables. The dishes that were not broken were used during the dinner. Daniel and Pete prepared the plates for everyone. Daniel wanted to limit the amounts that each person received. Under the circumstances, everyone seemed to be having a good time except Jezzy. She was angry at Pete. Pete was doing what he wanted and that got under her skin. He was supposed to be working for her. She didn't understand what he was doing. Pete felt that she was safe with this group of people and didn't need to be protected. Jezzy refused to talk during the meal. After she was finished eating, Pete pulled her aside to explain how he felt. He told her that this was her chance to be normal. She could interact with people without them wanting something from her. She never thought of it that way. Suddenly, Jezzy felt like a light was shining down on her. She was elated with the idea of being normal and not mauled by people. She gave Pete a big hug as if he had given her the biggest gift of all. Little did they know no one was very safe with a killer onboard.

*****

Tran spent most of the day watching Talina. He imagined how life would be living with her. Every time he fantasized being with her, he never thought about killing. That is, until he would hear Jasmine's voice. Seeing Talina giving her attention, his resentment against Jasmine deepened. After dinner, he sat up and leaned his head against the window at their booth. He closed his eyes and fell asleep. He quickly slipped into another nightmare. This time it was when he was very young. He couldn't remember how old he was, but the dream started with an event that would keep him a wake several nights. One day as he was coming home from school it was raining. In front of his house were big puddles filled with water. He jumped in the puddles while laughing loudly. He was having so much fun just being a kid. He forgot that his mother had just bought him new shoes from the dollar store. As he came into the trailer, he kicked off his shoes next to the door. It was a rule that if your shoes were wet, you had to leave them at the door. His mother didn't want him leaving tracks in the trailer. This day was different. When his mother got in, she came to his door with the thin blue dog leash that she had used before to beat him with. They had a dog for about a month before it ran away. She was screaming at Tran about how his new shoes were all muddy. Tran cried and said he was sorry but that didn't matter to her. She was so angry she started whipping him as hard as she could with the leash. The slashes cut through his soft pale skin like a knife. He was only wearing shorts and a tee-shirt. By the time she was done, he had blood marks all over his body. Most of the slashes were on his legs. Tran screamed in pain. It was just like the whipping slaves got back in the days. She stormed out of the room. Thirty minutes later she came back and all she could say is, "You know you deserved it." As an adult, he continued to have this dream.

*****

Since it was getting to be bedtime, the survivors took turns going to the bathroom in pairs. When everyone had finished they all agreed to blow out the candles they had lit earlier. Before they could think of sleeping, they asked Daniel why help had not arrived yet. He could only guess that since it was so windy all day, helicopters and planes could not get in the air yet. They were thankful that the light snow had fallen for a while, and then stopped. As they got quiet to try to sleep, they could hear some wildlife outside. Howling from the wolves frightened them the most. Some sounded too close for comfort. Later in the night, Jasmine awoke and decided to go to the bathroom. She was half awake so she didn't think to take someone with her. Tran was awake and watched Jasmine as she went out the door. The urge to follow was too great, so he grabbed his bag and quietly followed her. Tran needed a fix and his resentment of her gave him the motivation to get rid of her. It had been several days since his last kill. It was difficult to see in the dark so he listened to the sound of her footsteps as she walked through the snow. He didn't want to use a flashlight because she might see him following her. Jasmine stopped for a moment.

"Is someone there?" Jasmine asked as she found her spot.

Tran didn't reply.

Jasmine squatted down to relieve herself. She listened for any noise that would indicate danger. Tran quietly approached her from behind. Jasmine stood and pulled her pants up. As she turned to walk back to the dining car, she found herself face to face with Tran.

"What are you doing here, Tran?" she indignantly demanded. She felt a more than little angry that he had invaded her privacy. Jasmine was also unsettled by his presence. Something was off with him. She wasn't sure if she should be afraid.

Suddenly, without saying a word, Tran threw her down to the ground and jumped on top of her.

"Tran, what are you doing?" Jasmine pleaded. He realized he had to silence her quickly. He threw his hands around her throat before she could scream. Jasmine's eyes widened as she realized he was seriously hurting her. She kicked violently, trying to throw Tran off her. He wanted to get rid of her so he would have Talina all to himself. He thought he could be Talina's best friend. As he tightened his grip on Jasmine's throat, he could see her eyes from the light of the moon. Jasmine tried to cry out but couldn't. Tears started streaming down her face as she couldn't understand why Tran was doing this. She fought as hard as she could, but she felt that she was losing the fight. At that moment, she realized he was trying to kill her. He could see Jasmine's eye lids start to relax as her body became lifeless. He continued to hold onto her neck. After a couple minutes, he slowly slipped off her body and sat next to her while catching his breath. Jasmine was now dead. Tran reached into his bag to get his headphones. As he turned on his favorite song, he took the metal back scratcher out of the bag. He flipped Jasmine's body over and pulled her shirt up. Tran closed his eyes and lost himself in the song that gave him a high like no other. His body felt like it was lifting off the ground. With his right hand gripping the back scratcher, he opened his eyes and violently started tearing the skin on her back. Each stroke was harder than the last. This time was different. Tran was angry about being stuck in the wilderness, so he tore Jasmine's back with forcible anger. As the song ended he realized the job was done. He sat back and noticed he had a little blood on his shirt. How would

Cat Scratch Killer

he explain this? Tran quickly wiped off the scratcher with part of Jasmine's shirt. He put everything back in his bag and quietly returned to the dining car.

Talina saw Tran come in from outside. "Where have you been?"

"Just going to the bathroom," he replied.

Since Talina and Jasmine slept back to back, she didn't notice that Jasmine was missing. It was difficult to see in the dark dining car. A little light was coming in from the full moon and clear skies. Talina thought she noticed Tran with his bag but didn't question him. It seemed like he never left his bag out of sight. It was too dark for her to notice the blood on his shirt.

As daylight broke, a few started to wake up. Jezzy sat up and starting whining about the fact that they had not been rescued yet.

Zack woke up a few feet from her. "Are you alright?" he asked with concern.

As she brought her hands down from her face, Jezzy quietly answered, "Yes, I just need to get it out before everyone wakes up. I'll try to be strong around the others," she responded.

"Well, I can go back to sleep if you need to cry some more," Zack said with a grin on his face.

Jezzy laughed, "No, I think I'm good."

Zack tried to lift Jezzy's spirits. "No problem. We'll get through this together," He patted her on the left shoulder.

71

As the dawn became morning, the rest of the group started to wake up.

Talina now noticed Jasmine was missing. "Has anyone seen Jasmine?" Talina desperately asked the others.

Some shook their heads, indicating that they had not seen her.

"Daniel, will you go with me to find Jasmine?" Talina asked.

"Sure, let's go," Daniel answered as he got up.

Talina wrapped herself with a tablecloth that was lying on the floor. "Maybe she went out for a bathroom break?"

As Daniel and Talina walked through the snow, Daniel got the feeling that something wasn't quite right.

"Wait, do you hear that?" Daniel said as he stopped Talina.

"Sounds like growling," Talina answered.

Suddenly they both could see through the brush there were some wolves devouring something. They couldn't make out what it was. Talina took a step closer and quickly put her hands to her mouth as she realized what they were eating. It was Jasmine. Daniel saw the horrified look on Talina's face. He quickly grabbed her hand and quietly led her back to the train car.

When they got back, Daniel made an announcement to the survivors, "Does anyone have a weapon?" he inquired.

Pete stood up, "Yes, I have a gun. It's for protection. Why?"

Daniel motioned for him to follow. "Come with me," he commanded.

As Daniel and Pete went outside, Talina continued to sob uncontrollably, barely able to explain to others what she had seen. Tran sat in his booth, watching her. He didn't feel bad about what he had done but he knew he would have to act like everyone else.

As Daniel led Pete to Jasmine's body, he explained what he and Talina had seen. Pete couldn't believe it until he saw it with his own eyes. He quickly took his gun out and fired it once in the air. He only wanted to scare off the wolves. The loud shot rang out as it echoed through the foothills. The wolves scattered in fear and ran off. Pete and Daniel slowly approached Jasmine's body. The wolves devoured so much of Jasmine's back that they couldn't see the scratch marks Tran left. In fact, it looked like she was killed by the wolves. They both stood over her in disbelief.

Daniel knelt down, turned Jasmine over and picked up her body. He put her in the engine car, along with the waiter and the engineer who were killed during the avalanche while Pete kept his gun drawn in case the wolves came back. When Daniel and Pete went back into the dining car, they could see most of the survivors tearing up after hearing the news. Daniel explained to everyone that Jasmine was deceased and was placed in the engine car for safe keeping.

Tran couldn't have been more relieved that they didn't figure out he killed her. He could still keep his secret. For the first time, Tran realized how he affected other lives with his actions. Talina seemed helpless and bawled uncontrollably. He wanted to reach out to her but guilt overcame him. How could he ever make this up to her? He couldn't! However, he couldn't take his eyes off her. How could he bring so much pain to someone he cared about? At that point he wanted to kill himself. He had to say something to her but what? The mood was somber as most of the survivors ate dry cereal for breakfast. As they finished, they all sat in silence. Tran got up and sat next to Talina.

"Are you ok?" he asked with concern.

"No, I will never be ok after today," Talina stonily replied. Her words drove a knife into Tran's heart. There was nothing he could do or say.

"I'm so sorry Talina," Tran said.

"Tran, I don't want to be rude, but I just don't have it in me to talk right now," Talina told in a soft voice.

"I understand," Tran responded sadly. He reflected on the fact that he never had a best friend, and that he probably would have had those kinds of feelings if anything bad ever happened to them.

Cat Scratch Killer

He had acquaintances in the past but not very close friends. Tran realized how lucky Talina was to have someone to care about her like that. He also realized how caring Talina really was. He vowed at this point not to do anything to ever hurt Talina again, and if he could, he would always protect her. Despite the short time he had known Talina he realized he was in love with her.

Chapter 5 – Rescue and Survival

Everyone kept to themselves for the next hour. Then, John could hear something very familiar. He had lived near an airport when he was younger. "Hey, hey, I think I hear a helicopter. Everyone ran outside except for Arthur, Doris and Tran.

The group gazed up at the sky to see if anything was flying over. Suddenly, Dennis shouted, "There! It's a helicopter!" He pointed to a helicopter coming just over the foothill near their setting.

Frantically jumping up and down, and waving their hands, each person tried to flag down the helicopter. They noticed a package being dropped over the tracks in front of the engine car. After the helicopter dropped the package, it turned and left. Disappointment registered as they realized this was not going to be a rescue. They sprinted through the snow to retrieve it.

"Zack, can you help me carry this? Pete asked. "We can open it in the dining car."

Zack squatted, "Sure, it's kind of exciting to see what they sent."

As Pete and Zack carried the large, heavy box back to the train, the others followed. When they got inside, Daniel got a sharp knife from the kitchen. He began to pry the carton open as all eyes anxiously watched him. As he opened the top, he took out a letter that lay on top. He handed it to Dennis.

Dennis quickly scanned it to see if he could share it with the rest. When he could see that it was good news, he read the letter out loud, "A rescue mission is being assembled and will be sent out early tomorrow morning when the skies are clear and the winds are expected to be low." He paused to let the news sink in, then continued, "Make a number in the snow to let us know how many survivors need to be rescued. The helicopter will be back in an hour to see the number. It will be a swift rescue. Please be advised, another snow storm is coming through the next night so we need to do a rescue as quickly as possible. We will then investigate the crash after the next storm blows over."

Daniel had a big smile on his face as he pulled out blankets, candles, lighters, water, rations of food, flashlights and batteries. A radio was provided for communication if someone needed immediate medical attention. The mood was infinitely more positive now that they knew a rescue would be coming soon.

Tran wasn't so sure this was good news for him. He didn't know how he could keep under the radar with all the publicity that was about to come. Sitting quietly he watched as everyone else celebrated with excitement and tried to imagine how the rescue would go. He had already decided that he would decline on camera interviews. Since he needed medical attention, it might delay anyone who would try to get a statement from him.

Zack came up with a great idea to kill time. "Hey, remember all the old TV show songs? Why don't we sing a few? I can start with the Brady Bunch theme."

Jezzy turned around to Zack and started laughing, "You are too funny, Zack. But it is a way to make the time go by."

To keep the mood positive, the group joined in singing and laughing. Pete motioned to Jezzy that he needed to talk to her. She got up and came over to the booth he was sitting in. He suggested that they volunteer to go out and make the survivor number in the snow. She agreed, so they told Daniel, "We were going out to make the number for the helicopter to find."

The rest of the group was too busy having fun to notice where Pete and Jezzy were going. As Pete took Jezzy outside, he talked to her about how great she was doing with not being hounded by fans and media. She told him that it was the best time she had in a long time. She really felt like a normal person. He suggested she plan a trip once a year to get away from everything. She liked the thought of the idea very much. Jezzy and Pete cleared a patch of snow behind the train cars. Then they gathered wood to form the number twelve. Their hands were freezing cold by the time they were done. It took them almost a half an hour to complete the job. When they got back inside, the group was still singing, so Pete and Jezzy joined in the fun after they warmed up their hands.

*****

But Tran wasn't in the mood for singing. His mind continued to go back to the past. He started thinking about when he was 9 years old. He remembered that one day his mother locked him out of the trailer while she was with a man. Tran was out playing with his friends. They were playing a game called "Stop and Go." As he was running up behind one of his friends during the game, his friend's elbow hit the bottom of his jaw, causing Tran to bite his tongue all the way through. Blood started pouring out of his mouth. He started crying due to the pain.

He ran home, and held his right hand to his mouth as the blood continued to pour out. He banged on the trailer door for his mom to answer. He continued crying when no one would answer the door. The feeling of abandonment took over. He then started screaming for someone to answer. Finally, his mother came to the door. She opened the sliding glass door and led him to the kitchen sink. She held his mouth under the kitchen spigot. As the cool water eased the pain, Tran stopped crying. Jackie grabbed an ice pack from the freezer." What happened out there?" she asked. As he explained what happened, his mother lit a cigarette. She acted nervous as Tran tried to explain.

"Hey, what's taking so long?" The man interrupted from the other room.

"Hold your horses!" Jackie shouted back. She looked at Tran and said, "You're going to be all right. Stop acting like it's a big deal." she said with a smirk on her face. This just confirmed that Tran was alone in this world.

Jackie got up and went into the other room and finished having sex with her trick. She left the cigarette burning in the ashtray. Tran picked it up and took a small puff from it. He coughed until he almost choked. Then he ran to his room, crying until he fell asleep. When he woke up, his mother sat in the living room watching TV, smoking another cigarette. "Well, you finally decided to wake up," she rudely remarked to him. He realized he would not get any sympathy from her. He felt alone, sad, angry and empty. When these feelings resurfaced from time to time, Tran would have the urge to kill.

*****

John and Dennis decided to go out for a bathroom and smoke break. John took the gun just in case they needed it. Each time a pair went out for a bathroom break one person would carry the loaded gun.

Cat Scratch Killer

The men walked a short distance down the tracks behind the dining car. They found an area in the trees to the right that was uphill. As they were doing their business, they could feel a presence among them. There was something creeping in the brush and watching their every move. It had eyes of gold that pierced through the night. The wild animal locked eyes on one individual, John. Suddenly, a panther lunged out at him. Neither saw it coming. As the panther jumped at John, he began screaming. The panther locked his jaw on the sleeve of his shirt, shredding the fabric, and tearing the flesh of his lower arm. With his right hand, he reached in his pocket and pulled out the gun. Trying to aim at the panther, he was thrashing around too much to pull the trigger. He threw the gun away from his body onto the ground.

"Shoot him! Shoot him! Dennis, shoot him!" John screamed as his arm continued to be torn apart by the vicious panther.

Dennis dove towards the gun and pointed it at the panther. He couldn't get a clear shot with John fighting. Dennis cried out, "I got it. I'm trying to aim without hitting you."

John continued to struggle, getting weaker by the moment. "Shoot him! I can't hold him much longer!"

Dennis kept waving the gun around. "I'm trying. I can't get a clear shot!"

Suddenly, everything started to happen in slow motion. Dennis saw a clear shot. He fired the gun directly into the back of the panther's neck.

John screamed out as the bullet took off his lower left ear lobe. The bullet traveled through the panther's neck and landed in the dirt.

"Shit, Shit! Did you have to take off my ear?" John yelled out while throwing the dead panther off his body.

"I'm sorry. You both kept moving around!" Dennis yelled back.

"Yeah, I was trying to fight off a damn panther!" John continued yelling in panic. Blood continued to drip from his arm and ear.

Pete, Zack and Daniel came running out of the dining car. At first, they didn't know which direction to run. Then, they could hear John yelling at Dennis. As they ran towards them, they saw the dead panther on the ground. The men were in disbelief that such a wild animal was living in these parts of the woods.

Pete looked at John and could see the blood splatters on the ragged fabric of his shirt sleeve. "Oh my God, John! Your arm!" he exclaimed.

John looked down at his arm, "Yeah, he got me good. I would have been a dead man if Dennis weren't here." Then, with grateful eyes, he apologized to Dennis. "Hey man, I'm sorry for getting upset with you. I just freaked out."

Dennis shook his head back and forth, in response. "No John, you don't need to apologize. I would have freaked out too. Let's get you inside before you go into shock so our girls can take care of that arm. Oh, and sorry about the ear," he added. They both laughed in spite of the situation as they started walking back to the dining car.

Suddenly, Zack stopped for a moment. Pete turned back to see why Zack stopped.

"Should we save that animal for meat?" Zack asked.

Pete tilted his head to the left while he thought for a moment. "I don't think we need to. Since we got more food, I think we are good."

Zack looked at Pete. "Would if the rescue doesn't go as planned and we are here longer than expected?"

Pete started walking back towards the panther. "Yep, you've got a point. We should save him just in case. Good thinking," Pete commented.

The men picked up the panther and took it to the engine car to add it to the bodies of Jasmine, the other engineer, and the waiter.

As John and the other men returned to the dining car, Talina realized that she was the only one that knew how to give first aide. Talina sewed up John's arm but he had a lot of deep cuts and laceration injuries. Since most of his arm was affected, she used some bandages but also used a clean towel to wrap his arm. The whole time she worked on John, he never made a sound about the pain.

*****

Tran watched Talina care for John's wounds. He started thinking about his childhood and how he hated his mother. He reflected on a day he was sick at home. He vomited on the floor in his bedroom. His mother stormed into his room, yanked him out of bed and as he lay on the floor in his own vomit, she kicked him in the stomach. He couldn't breathe for a few seconds. She then pulled him to his closet and shoved him inside. "I'm tired of you waking me up." She yelled as she continued punching him. Suddenly, the door slammed with him inside. It was completely dark. He felt safer inside but scared of the loneliness. He was only eight years old. He cried himself to sleep, cramped and lying on top of a few toys. The need to go to the bathroom overwhelmed him. Tran beat on the door trying to get out but his mother had blocked the door with a chair. Daylight came in from under the door. He began to cry again when he realized that his underwear had become soiled. It had been hours since he had been thrown in the closet. He could hear the school bus outside his apartment so he figured it was about 8:05 am. Tran tried imagining he was with his grandmother to make the time go by. Suddenly, the door opened. "Get out of there and get yourself something to eat," his mother said as she walked away. He got up and grabbed a clean pair of underwear from his drawer. He went to the bathroom to wash up. He rinsed his soiled underwear out in the bathroom sink so his mother would not get mad at him. He hung them up to dry in his closet and cleaned up the remaining mess on the floor of the closet. Feeling sick to his stomach, he got dressed and went to the kitchen. Tears fell from his face. "Mom, I'm really sick." Tran pleaded. Jackie stood up from her chair, "God Damn it! Fine, stay home but I don't want to see you out of your room. Keep your door shut!" Tran had just enough energy to go back to his room, close the door and climb back in bed. The vomit was not cleaned up until the next day.

*****

"You sure are quiet," Talina remarked to Tran.

"Yeah, I'm just zoning out I guess," Tran answered.

"Is your leg still hurting?" Talina asked with concern.

"Only when I'm thinking about it," Tran joked.

"Oh, sorry I brought it up." Talina smiled.

The group was passing time doing their own thing. Bobby and Brayden were in a booth and began playing Tic Tac Toe on paper. Brayden loved playing games with his dad.

Daniel and Pete decided to go in the kitchen and make an easy lunch for everyone. Doris and Arthur decided to take a nap after they fed Trinity and let her go to the bathroom. Dennis, Zack and John talked in a booth at the very end near the door that led outside.

Jezzy and Talina decided to take a bathroom break. Jezzy carried the gun. She learned how to use a gun when she was a child. Her father was a cop and would take her to the gun range, letting her practice when she was turned sixteen. Jezzy and Talina decided to walk in front of the two train cars. They looked for an area of trees to go to the bathroom. As Talina was starting to go to the bathroom, she could hear something in the brush. As she looked in the direction where the wrestling sounds came from, she could see something small moving but it was too deep in the brush to make out what it was. Talina continued to watch the bushes, but not telling Jezzy what she was looking at. Suddenly, it hopped out towards her. Talina jumped and realized it was just a rabbit that didn't know she was there. As Talina jumped, the rabbit also got scared and ran off.

"Talina, are you ok?" Jezzy shouted.

"Yeah, it was just a rabbit. It scared the crap out of me." Talina answered with a nervous laugh. They both walked back with relief that it was a false scare. They agreed not to tell the group since it would make them nervous during bathroom breaks.

When Jezzy and Talina returned, Doris decided she couldn't sleep and wanted to get to know Jezzy a little better. She asked her how she started her career. While Talina, Tran, John, Zack and Dennis listened, Jezzy explained that she started modeling when she was thirteen. She was discovered at a movie theatre by an agent. She started doing local commercials, then ads for local department stores. It wasn't long before she was getting work with magazines. The one thing she had no interest in was runway modeling. She was always afraid of falling until she met a runway model at a magazine shoot. She learned that it was easy and fast money. When she was fifteen, her mother hired a trainer to help her learn the skills and walk needed for the runway. By the time she was sixteen, she was a household name. It was no surprise. She was a beautiful brunette with hair down to her waist, 5'7" and thin. She tanned easily and her skin had a beautiful glow. Jezzy's eyes were hazel which was very rare to find in models. Her nose was a little narrow, but her lips were pink and perfect. She was easy to look at.

*****

While some listened to Jezzy's story, Tran reflected on a night when his mother shoved him into a kitchen cabinet and told him to stay there while she had a trick knocking on the door. He remembered the darkness and how scared he was in the small space. Not knowing when he would be able to come out. Not knowing if the man she was with would hurt him just like her drug dealer did. His thoughts ran rabid as he reflected how it felt to be a little boy in the dark scary space. *Why is my mom making me hide in the dark? Why isn't it okay for that man to know that I am here? I must be a bad person. I must be a terrible person if she doesn't want anybody to know that I belong to her. She hates me. I know she hates me. What did I ever do to make her hate me so much? Do all kids go through this? Are children put in a dark space and left to feel scared? I know that the cabinet door could open at any second and mom will start hitting me again. Or will it be that man my mom is with and is he going to hurt me?* As Tran continued to remember how he felt as a child, he remembered the sounds his mother would make when she was having sex. The screaming that she would do. This was all too familiar. Tran could feel anger rising in his blood at that moment. Forgetting his surroundings in the woods while waiting for rescue to come, he was consumed by the memory of it. All Tran could think of was how much hatred he had for his mother. Everything she had done to him. *That bitch deserved to die. I wish I could kill her over and over again.*

Psychologists would say those women he killed represented his mother, but Tran couldn't put the two together. Suddenly, he had the urge to kill again. He yearned for that feeling of euphoria right now. The problem was everyone huddled together in one area waiting to be rescued. *Besides, I already killed one of them. Killing another one of them would be too suspicious. I just have to fight these feelings until I can kill again.*

"It's nearing one o'clock, who is ready for lunch?" Daniel announced. "Help yourselves. There are sandwiches and chips in the kitchen."

It didn't take long before everyone grabbed a sandwich and chips to eat. While they ate, Zack had the radio on and tuned to a station that reported news all day. The topic of the day centered on the daring rescue that was planned for them the next morning. The announcer gave enough details to help the survivors keep faith that they would be rescued soon.

Talina sat down next to Tran, using this opportunity to get to know him a little better. "What are you going to do when you get home?"

"Well, actually I don't have a home to go to."

"Why?"

"I wanted a new start so I decided to take the train to a new place. I have always wanted to go to Salt Lake City. But I'm starting to miss St. Louis so I might go back." Tran lied. He told her this only because he knew she lived there and he fantasized about a life with her.

Talina got quiet for a moment. She pondered the thought of having Tran as a roommate since Jasmine was no longer with her. "Tran, maybe you could stay with me. Jasmine was my roommate. Now that she is....is...no longer here, I have an opening in my apartment. So, what do you think?" Talina finished.

Tran could not believe what he was hearing. How could he respond with a hundred thoughts rushing through his mind? He never imagined things moving this fast and for her to be the one to instigate things. "I like that idea!" he blurted without thinking as his face lit up with excitement.

"Well then, that settles it. We are now roommates!" Talina proclaimed. She extended her hand out to shake with Tran.

"Hey, can you excuse me for a minute?" Tran suddenly asked as he got up and slowly walked towards the door. He limped outside to a secluded area where he could think for a while. *Oh my God, what am I getting myself into? There is no way I can live with Talina and for her not to figure out who I am. I can wear a mask most the time, but I don't know if I'm really that good to be able to live with somebody and keep that mask on all the time. And what if we get in an argument? I don't want to hurt her, but I don't know what I would do if I got angry at her. I don't know what I'm capable of even to a person that I care about. I have never felt this before for anyone. I don't know how to deal with these feelings. Damn it. If she really knew who I was. If she really knew what I've done. How would I know that she would not go to the police? How could I get rid of these thoughts of wanting to kill somebody?*

Cat Scratch Killer

I don't have the urge to kill near as much as I usually do. But still, the urge could be there any time. I wish I could kill right now to get it out of my system. I need to have that feeling of being in control again. For the past couple days, I haven't been in control of anything. The thought of moving in with her could almost be out of my control. How can I move in with her and still be in control? She's going to expect me to go out and get a job. How can I do that when I don't have any identification? I have been living in the streets for so long. That's what I'm used to. How do I really expect to pull this off? I'm not a normal person. There's no way I can go out and get a job like normal people. The thought of paying bills and helping her pay rent is crazy. I don't even know what it is to make a living. Yeah, I've heard the phrase but when you have been out on the streets for as long as I have, those words don't even make sense. This is my chance to be normal but I don't know if it's too late for me. I have to do this. I must find a way to get a job where I don't have to have a bank account or paychecks. Where I can just get paid in cash and still be able to help her with rent and bills? I just hope I can do this and most of all, I hope I don't hurt her. I know what I'm capable of.

As Tran pondered these thoughts, his body shivered from the cold. The pain from his knee was now so intense that he hobbled back inside to Talina.

"You're really hurting, aren't you?" Talina asked. "You must be really cold. You were out there for quite a while."

"Yeah, I think my knee is swelling up more," Tran responded.

Talina looked at him with concern. "When I was nine years old I fell out of a tree and broke my arm. It hurt so much I thought I was going to die. I had a good doctor though. He was very gentle and seemed like he cared. I had to wear that cast for six weeks. I hated it!" Talina added while trying to take Tran's mind off his pain.

"Did you like climbing trees when you were young?" Tran asked.

"I loved it. That was the other thing. I couldn't climb trees with that darn cast."

Zack joined Talina and Tran. "I am actually paying for a cabin in Salt Lake City right now. I have two weeks. I can't wait to get there and take a nice hot shower and sleep in a soft bed," Zack bragged.

"Oh, and you're inviting us to stay with you?" Talina teased. She thought Zack was kind of cute but knew she needed to get back to her job interview once they all got rescued.

As it got dark, Doris lit candles so it would be easier to see. They all gathered in a circle and shared stories of their favorite Christmas when they were younger. Tran spent one Christmas with his grandmother. It was probably the only Christmas he could remember that he was happy. He never understood why his mother didn't just let him go live with her all the time.

Then Jezzy shared an interesting story. One Christmas, her dad's police department donated nice used toys to homeless kids. "My father told me that for every nice toy I donated, I would get a new toy for Christmas. I decided to donate ten toys, since I was ten years old. My dad got such a kick out of my idea. He ended up giving me eleven Christmas presents. You know, one to grow on. The kicker was, when he showed me the eleventh gift, he rolled out a brand new dark purple bike with a white sparkle banana seat. I was so happy that I cried tears." That was a Christmas she never forgot.

The night passed very slowly. As the sunrise came, everyone was left on their own to eat what they wanted. When a couple hours had passed, everyone started looking at their watches, checking them every few minutes. It was only half past seven but each person was filled with anticipation of being rescued.

Finally John spoke up "I think I hear something. Hush, quiet, listen, do you hear that?"

Everyone ran outside. Then, from a far distance you could hear sounds of helicopters. Two military helicopters appeared over the trees.

"Yes, it's about time!" Zack shouted.

"I am so ready to go home!" Talina's voice was bursting with joy. With a huge smile, she turned to Tran and continued, "And you are going to start a new life."

Tran smiled back.

At that point, Bobby turned to Daniel, "Daniel, thank you so much for everything you did."

Doris walked up to Daniel. "You have no idea how we appreciate it. You know, you're a hero."

Daniel smiled, "I am grateful to have gotten to know all of you." He explained what he expected to happen when the rescue ended. "I'm sure there's going to be reporters and a lot of people asking a lot of questions. I wish we could have saved everybody. Talina deserves credit. She really did a good job patching us up." Daniel turned to Talina and added, "I am so sorry about your friend, Jasmine."

Arthur stood up. "Daniel sometimes we just don't know what God's plan is and maybe you weren't meant to save everyone. But you both did a darn good job saving us!" Arthur said with a big smile.

"You got that right," Doris said as she hugged her husband. At that moment, everyone started hugging each other. The realization sunk in that this was probably going to be the last time they would see each other.

Cat Scratch Killer

As the helicopters flew over the trees, coming closer and closer, everyone felt relief. Tran, however, was filled with several emotions. Talina noticed he was unusually quiet and seemed very detached from the scene unfolding around him.

*****

The mild pain medication seemed to have no effect on his knee. It was throbbing, so he started thinking back to when he was a child. This time he could remember as far back as two years old. His mother was living with a man named Darren. Darren and Tran got along so well, people thought that Darren was Tran's father. When Darren's grandmother passed away, leaving him a small inheritance, he came home with a new blue pickup truck. Tran loved riding around town with Darren. He often imagined himself driving a nice truck later in life.

Darren was a nice, good-looking man. He and Jackie had met at a local pub, six months after Tran was born. Soon after they started dating, Darren had moved in with Jackie and Tran. They fought a lot but Tran could tell that they loved each other. Darren was a construction worker so he was in shape. During the winter season when Tran became three years old, it was hard for Darren to find work. Jackie was a waitress at a local diner.

On Christmas Eve, Darren had been out late and came home drunk. There was a smudge of lipstick on his shirt and the smell of cheap dime store perfume. Tran lay in his bed, trying to go to sleep. He could hear his mother screaming at Darren. She was tired of having to pay most of the bills and now he had been sleeping with another woman. Suddenly, Tran's door flew open and his mother was screaming, "Get up. Tran, we're leaving." Tran was confused about what was going on.

"Where are we going, mommy?" Tran asked.

"I don't know, Tran, anywhere but here." Jackie responded as she opened the closet door and pulled out some of Tran's clothes. She ran out of the room and a couple minutes later came back in with empty grocery bags and started filling them up with Tran's clothes. Tran started crying as he realized that they were leaving Darren. This was the only father figure that he had ever had. As Jackie was gathering Tran's clothes, Darren had gone to their room and passed out. She started taking their clothes and putting them in the truck. "This is Darren's truck, why are we taking it?" Tran asked his mother.

"We won't need it very long. Now get in the truck." Jackie answered as she got into the driver seat and started the engine. As they were pulling away, Tran looked back for the last time at the small house holding mixed memories. He had no idea that this would change the course of his life becoming the nightmare he would know for years.

As Jackie was driving, she started crying, ranting out loud about how Darren betrayed her and that he was a loser. Tran put his hands up over his ears to try to block out what his mother was saying about the man he had so much respect for. Tears were falling down his face as he realized that he would never see Darren again. Jackie didn't have anywhere to go. She pulled into a store parking lot. "We need to get some sleep. I'm not sure where we are going to live now." Jackie said. She was scheduled to work the next day early in the morning. It was freezing cold outside and sleeping was difficult to do while trying to stay warm. Jackie only needed to work a half shift since it was Christmas day.

*****

Weather conditions had subsided enough to attempt the rescue. Every rescue is an attempt and the plans involved two helicopters which assigned the survivors into groups. Those needing immediate care were consigned to Helicopter Emergency Medical Services (HEMS for short) aboard an Eagle 407. The rest were given a ride in a Bell 212 Helicopter.

As the first pilot landed the Bell 212 chopper, a strong wind draft and unstable snowpack made it too risky to power down. So with the blades still whirring, producing a flurry of re-circulating snow which reduced visibility, the first group of survivors fought their way to the helicopter door.

Zack, Dennis, Pete, Jezzy, Brayden, Bobby and Daniel were introduced to Lieutenant Roberts who was flying them to the closest airport which happened to be Denver International.

Representatives from the railroad had some questions for them as well. A railroad spokesperson cautioned the media before letting crews do a live news conference with them and short individual interviews. After they gave their statements, the railroad paid for lodging and flights back to their home towns.

The Eagle 407 took the most critically injured directly to the University Hospital in Denver. The MedEvac team provided advanced prehospital care onboard to Tran, John and Arthur. Talina answered questions concerning each one's specific trauma since she had attended to their injuries. Doris was tasked with keeping Trinity in her crate until they arrived on the helipad. They ignored questions from the media while being rushed into the ER.

The bodies in the engine locomotive and the other cars would be recovered later. As both helicopters lifted off the ground everyone took one last look down to the thick forest remembering these last few days. As they rose to a higher altitude, they could see the mountain that had caused the avalanche, and the wreckage of the derailed train cars, and more. It looked like a toy train that fell off its track. The beautiful white snow blanketed most of the wreckage, covering the tragedy that would haunt some of the survivors for years.

It was a somber moment as they comprehended that some people who had lost their lives were still on the train. Feeling the sadness, everyone quietly gazed down on the disastrous wreck.

This would be in the history books. The grim truth was they had survived such a tragedy. It would change their lives forever.

*****

Tran needed minor knee surgery. He didn't have ID so he told them that he lost his ID in the train wreck. Talina gave them her address since Tran was going to live with her. Surgery was done late that afternoon and Tran was released the next day with the understanding it was important for him to get complete bed rest for the next couple weeks. Talina had gone to a hotel that night while Tran stayed overnight at the hospital. She gave herself a quick wash up and went to bed. She was too tired to take a full shower and wash her hair. The next day, she ate a big breakfast before going back to the hospital. Tran was being released to go home that day. Doris, Arthur and John received discharge clearance a few days later and were given tickets to fly back to their home towns. Media requests for information were denied until lawyers for the railroad could talk to the passengers, pending further investigation. This made Tran very relieved.

Talina agreed to let Tran live with her rent free in St. Louis for the next couple months while his knee healed. She also paid for his pain medications. Talina saved money any chance she got. Her parents helped her with college and expenses because they knew she wouldn't squander the cash. She had about $9,000 in her savings account. Talina would take odd jobs that didn't lock her into a schedule. That way, it wouldn't conflict with her school schedule. She had been thrifty ever since she was 14 years old babysitting for neighbors.

Talina was ready to take part in a new journey of her life. Now out of school, she was about to become a nurse. The past couple days gave her some practice but now she was about to experience the real thing. Her life, her daydreams, thoughts about her career and how it would start right after school had included Jasmine. Now there was no Jasmine.

Tran and Talina took a flight later that next day after Tran's surgery. They were both so exhausted they fell asleep on the plane. When Talina finally opened the door to her apartment, she led Tran into a home he had never had before. For the first time in his life, home was safe. She had never had a male roommate before, but this actually felt good to her. Tran seemed a little shy, however, that didn't seem to bother her. It would be a challenge to bring him out of his shell. She trusted Tran even though she hadn't known him very long. Talina thought about doing a background check and trying to get references, but decided against it after all they'd been through.

Chapter 6 – New Beginnings

As they arrived at Talina's apartment, Tran waited in the living room while Talina went into Jasmine's room and respectfully put her things in boxes. Suddenly, Tran could hear Talina crying. He contemplated if he should check to see if she was ok or would that be over doing it? As he got up and limped down the hall, he looked inside the bedroom, "Hey, are you okay?"

Talina looked up with red rimmed eyes sniffling, and said, "Yes, I just need to get this out."

Tran turned around and went back into the living room. He stood there for a moment then looked in the kitchen. He hobbled to the refrigerator to see if there was anything to drink. He took a soda from the second shelf and went back to the living room. As Tran sat down, he could hear Talina's crying getting louder. To drown it out, he grabbed a television remote and turned the TV on.

As he flipped through the channels, Talina walked in. "I'm going to get a quick shower and wash this crap out of my hair.

Make yourself at home since this is your home. Your room is ready." She smiled feebly and walked back to her bedroom. Her apartment had two bathrooms and she had the master bedroom that had an adjoining bathroom. There was a main bathroom in the hallway across from the guest bedroom. This would be the bathroom that Tran would use. Tran could not remember the last time he had a good hot shower. He thought this was a great idea. So, he went to his bedroom with his gym bag and got his other clothes out. They were not as dirty as the clothes he had on. He went into the main bathroom to get a shower. He could hear Talina's shower going. He liked the idea of taking a shower at the same time she was taking one. Hopefully, someday they would take a one together, but the thought did not last long when her water turned off a few seconds later. He finished his shower, got dressed and came back out. Talina should have been out of her room, but she wasn't. He went to the kitchen to make something for lunch. There was bread and cheese in the refrigerator. The bread was not as soft as he would have liked. It was not moldy so he decided to make grilled cheese sandwiches with some butter that was also in the fridge. Tran quickly got to know his way around the kitchen. There were some boxes of dry food in the pantry. Opening the cabinet doors, he located pots and pans. Tran daydreamed about Talina, thinking they would make a good couple. *This is nice. I could get used to this. It's been a long time since I cooked. I forgot how much I like it.* He remembered a Shania Twain love song video and he daydreamed of romantic relationship images with him and Talina.

Remembering how his grandmother made simple things, like grilled cheese sandwiches which were his favorite, brought a small smile to his face. As he was finishing, Talina came out of her room.

She immediately smelled the aroma of the sandwiches. "Wow that smells great." Talina said as she walked up to Tran with red rimmed eyes.

"Well, I figured you would be hungry."

"Thanks, Tran. I am a little hungry." Talina took a sandwich and walked into the living room. "Did you find something to watch?"

"No, it's all yours." Tran put one sandwich on his plate and cut in half the last sandwich leaving a half for Talina just in case she was still hungry. He went into the living room and sat down in the chair as Talina was sitting on the couch. They began watching TV shows together. At times, he would look at her and just enjoy being in the same room with her. He was falling more in love by the minute. After they finished eating, Tran felt tired and his leg was hurting. He did not want to go back to the hospital as he had no money, so he just wanted his knee to heal on its own. "I'm going to go lay down for a while. I'm a little tired and my leg is hurting."

Talina looked up at him, "Ok. Let me know if you need anything."

He went into his room, closed the door, lay down and quickly fell asleep. Talina watched a little more TV, which made her tired as well. After cleaning up the kitchen, she went into her room shut the door, laid down and soon fell into a deep sleep as well.

As the days went by, Tran realized that he needed to get a job. It would make him feel like a man to help Talina with the bills. His knee wasn't as swollen now so he called around to jobs relating to yard work and found a man just starting his own company. Tran asked the man to pay him cash, explaining that he finally had a new address. His employer would pay him every couple days for his work. If it worked out, he would get paid in cash every two weeks on Friday. Tran could buy some clothes from a thrift store to save money and help Talina with expenses. It was a good feeling that he could support himself. When Talina and Tran were not working, they spent a lot of time with each other. Sometimes they went to the movies, out to eat, grocery shopping together, or hanging out at the mall for fun. Sometimes they would go to the park and just hang out on the bench and watch other people. In Tran's mind, they were forming memories of falling in love. For Talina, she was just hanging out with her new friend and roommate. She had no plans for a relationship because she wanted to focus on her career.

One night they got into an argument. It was about a month after becoming roommates. They were both watching TV, sitting on the couch. Tran reached over and tried to kiss her. Talina jumped up and said, "Why did you do that Tran? You know, we are just roommates and friends. That's all it's ever going to be." Talina said.

Tran could feel rage building inside. It triggered the same rejection his mother gave him. When she indicated that she would never be in love with him, she stabbed his heart with a knife. He stood up and screamed at her. "How could I not fall in love with you, Talina?"

Talina didn't know what to say about that. She stormed off to her room and slammed the door. She realized that she was hurting his feelings, but Tran had to understand.

Tran was so angry he went to his room, grabbed his gym bag and stormed out of the apartment. He walked the streets in a fast motion. He was rambling to himself in anger. At that moment, he hated women again. It was time to kill. After walking several blocks, he saw a woman coming out the side of her house with the bag of trash. She walked down the few steps. Tran decided to approach her. He began to make small talk as she continued to walk towards her trash can. He looked around and realized there was no one that was watching. He grabbed her long hair with his right hand and put his left hand over her mouth. He dragged her to the back of the house. Once he got her to the back of the house, he wrapped his hands around her neck and started choking her while looking into her eyes. With the help of a dim porch light and the light of the moon, he could see the fear in her eyes as he squeezed hard. The light from her eyes faded as she became completely lifeless. He let her drop to the ground as he had always done. He then opened his bag and began his ritual. He turned her over, lifted her shirt, and got his recorder out from his bag. He placed the headsets on his ears and began listening to the music. He got the back scratcher and ripped the skin on her back. Suddenly, he wondered how this would affect her family. He started to wonder what her name was as he packed up his things. This was something he had never wondered before or cared about. Why would he care now? He didn't understand these feelings. He quickly left so as not to be caught. He kept wondering who the girl was. This time was different. Normally he would walk away feeling only the thrill.

When he got home, Talina came out of her room. "Tran, I'm sorry. You took me by surprise. Just, please don't do that again." As Talina was trying to apologize, Tran walked to his bedroom, threw his bag on his bed and shut his door.

Cat Scratch Killer

Tran was used to anger. That's all his mother showed ever him. To prevent Talina from hurting him anymore, he needed to close her out first. About an hour later, Tran went to the kitchen to grab a drink out of the fridge. He walked back to his room and shut the door again. He started crying. He didn't know how to act in front of Talina, now that she knew how he felt. His leg was hurting so he took his pain medications. The pain killers helped put him to sleep.

The next morning, Talina knocked on Tran's door. It was a Saturday so she was concerned that he was not up yet. When he didn't answer, she opened his door. He was gone. Tran left early to avoid a conversation of the night before. He ended up going to the park to think and sort out what he was going to say to Talina. Talina wasn't sure where Tran went. She knew he suffered from some untreated depression. This concerned her a great deal, after the disagreement they had the night before. Talina decided to go look for him. She knew it was too early for the theater to be open. They had recently gone grocery shopping so she didn't think he was at the store.

Talina decided to go to their favorite park. She didn't see him on the bench they normally sit on. She continued to walk on the trail that led thru the park. Then, she spotted Tran on the large swing set. Tran was bothered by Talina getting mad at him and started to obsess about his kill the night before. He wanted to know all about the woman he strangled. What was her name? What kind of family did she have? What kind of work did she do? This was out of character for him. It scared him. Usually, he didn't care about who the victim was.

As Talina was walking towards Tran, she stopped for a moment. She needed to gather her thoughts. She quickly came up with how she would approach him. She slowly walked towards the swings, and then sat on the swing next to him. He was sitting on a swing, staring at the ground with sad eyes.

Talina spoke first. "Hey, I came to make sure you are ok," She smiled to let him know she cared enough to be his friend.

Tran looked over at her. "Yeah, I just came out here to think."

Talina didn't want to talk about the night before either. She felt that she got her point across already. "Do you want to see a movie at the theater today?" she asked.

"Sure, that actually sounds like fun," he said. Tran felt his spirits start to lift as he felt accepted from Talina again. She started talking about a childhood memory. She was with a friend at the age of ten. It had snowed the night before. It ended up a snow day off from school. They were out enjoying the snow, and at one point, needed to cross a busy street. Watching for traffic, a moment came when they could run across. Talina had slipped and found herself in the middle of the road with traffic coming towards her. She could see a red pickup truck slamming on its breaks. The truck could not get traction and was sliding towards her. She tried to get up but it was too slick. As the truck was about to hit her, Talina's friend grabbed her and quickly dragged her to the other side of the road. She laid there in shock. The truck driver drove past her, and then pulled to the side of the road. A gentleman got out and walked towards the girls. He was checking to make sure they were not hurt. They were shaken up but no injuries. To this day it would sometimes haunt her in dreams.

Tran felt better now that Talina was sharing a moment with him. Now they made up, she would start having the same feelings he had. He decided to tell her one of his stories when he was young. "When I was at my grandmother's house in Florida, she would come out and talk to me while I was practicing on my skateboard. She really took an interest in my skateboarding by asking me if I wanted to enter skateboard competitions. I really didn't want to compete with anybody, I just liked skateboarding. My grandmother bought me a plain wood skateboard but said I could decorate it any way I wanted. I hung out with a couple of friends at times, and we would just skateboard for fun. When I was younger, grandmother also took me for swimming lessons."

Talina could tell how much Tran's grandmother loved him by all the activities she would do with him.

As they walked home Tran told her all the other special things his grandmother did for him. Later they went to the theater and saw a chick flick. The friendship seemed to be back on track but Tran continued to have obsessive feelings for Talina. She loved having a roommate that had time available to do things with. One thing did concern her though she didn't understand why Tran never wanted to get together with her and her friends. And he never invited her to join him with his friends. In fact, he never talked about having other friends. With all the time he was spending with her, how could he have time for any other friends? This wasn't a big deal for her right now, so she put it in the back of her mind for the time being. The next day was a Sunday. They went to the local mall and had so much fun. They sat on a bench and watched people walk by, picking out people they would like to date. Talina picked out guys that she thought were cute or might have a steady job. Tran picked out a couple girls but Talina did not see that those girls looked a lot like her. He didn't care that she was telling him the type of guys she would date. Just enjoying the time spent with her and laughing at the same time was enough for him. It became a regular routine going to the park, to the mall, to the movie theater, grocery shopping together, and sitting on the swings talking, or just running errands together. This was a perfect world for Tran however; the nights were still a problem for him. Nightmares from his childhood would haunt him, demanding a kill. On those nights, it felt like a heroin junkie needing a fix.

Monday evening, Talina came out to her car after work and discovered a note with a small package. The note claimed she would pay for rejecting his kindness but the note wasn't signed. She was hesitant to open the small box but wanted to see if this was a friend joking with her. She had a friend at work that like to pull pranks. As she slowly opened the box, she looked around to see if anyone was watching. When she didn't see anyone, she continued to tear off the wrapping on the box. She pried open the small box and discovered several photos of her. These photos showed her coming in and out of work on different days, working in the hospital halls and in the cafeteria, and other locations near home. Someone had to be following her. This was no prank.

Talina took the note and box of photos home and confided to Tran. "Tran, I discovered these crazy photos of me along with a note. I want your opinion. Should I go to the police with this? This stuff scares me."

"I don't think you need the police. I promise I'll make sure nothing ever happens to you. That guy will regret being born if I find out who is doing this to you." He reassured her in a soft tone of voice.

"Maybe I am making too much of it," she stated.

Christy Montgomery Michael

About two months after he had moved in with Talina, he woke up after having a terrible nightmare about his mother abusing him. He had so much rage inside of him. She always yelled at him to be the one to clean the trailer all the time. One night, she got angry at him and threw an ashtray full of ashes and butts. It hit him in the face and he had trouble breathing for several hours after.

Tran didn't have to go to work this morning and Talina was at work already. He didn't have a car so he walked down to the local market with his gym bag. A couple blocks from the market he could see a woman through the living room window of a house. It looked like she was vacuuming. Walking around the house, he peeked through the other windows to see if anyone else was in the house with her. When Tran didn't see anyone, he checked the back door. It was unlocked so he let himself in. He quietly hid in the kitchen to catch her off guard. The vacuum turned off. Her footsteps came closer towards the kitchen. He could feel the adrenaline in his heart speed up. She felt her hair being grabbed. Her head was jolted backwards by a force so strong it threw her down on the hard kitchen floor. Tran's dark figure quickly mounted her, putting his hands around her throat, squeezing her neck as hard as he could. She grabbed his arms and bucked her body to throw him off, but it did not work. She was fighting, and she was fighting hard. Looking deeply into her eyes, he tried to understand how she was feeling. Her skin was turning dark red, her lips turning blue. Slowly, her body became limp. The fight was over. He noticed a tear had rolled down from her left eye. He sat on top of her and just stared at her for nearly five minutes. This is something he had never done before. So many different things were running through his mind at the time. He wondered if anyone would care if she were dead or alive. If she had any children, any parents, a husband, siblings, close friends, anyone who would cry at her funeral. Her funeral, he had never been to a victim's funeral before. What that would be like? I should go this time. He then looked over, grabbed his bag and opened it. He took out his Walkman and placed the headsets over his ears, pushing the play button. Listening to his song, he thought about how Talina would have hated him for this. As he contemplated this, the familiar mechanical routine kicked in. The Cat Scratch Killer slowly rolled his victim over and pushed her shirt up. Pulling out the metal back scratcher, he tore into her skin. He made his mark several times methodically going across her back but slower this time. With each passing moment, Tran started to resent this kill. As the song ended he could feel his heart racing. Tears started falling down his face. Why was he crying? He hurriedly threw the back scratcher, Walkman and his headsets into the gym bag, zipped up the bag. This time, he wanted to know the name of his victim. He walked over to a desk that was in the living room and went through her mail. The name on the addressed mail read Heather Spazdon. Tran

ran out of the back door. Just to make sure that nobody saw him, he sprinted across two backyards, then walked out into the front yard of the second house. Tran made it to the sidewalk and strolled back to his apartment. He was pretty sure no one spotted him. That night the local news led with the story of the young mother killed in her home. From the description, he knew that this was his kill. The newscaster stated the name of the victim was being withheld, pending a police investigation.

When Talina came home, Tran was very quiet. He made a simple dinner for both of them.

"Are you feeling ok?" It seemed that Tran was in one of his moods again.

"I just felt a little tired," he answered her. "I think I'll go to bed early." Closing his door, he'd laid wake most of the night pondering about the woman he killed earlier that day. After Talina left for work the next morning he walked down to the local gas station and bought a newspaper. There was a full story on the killing with information on the funeral scheduled for a week later.

Tran decided that he would take the bus to the funeral. On that day he arrived early but waited across the street, and watched people go into the church. As the funeral was about to start, he crossed the street and entered the church. It was packed. He squeezed into a pew in the very back row. There were several large flower arrangements amid the victim and family photo display. Many people were crying.

It started with a couple of songs then the preacher got up and spoke. Apparently, this was her home church. The Pastor spoke lovingly of her, at times stopping to wipe tears away. Then a handsome gentleman stepped up and introduced himself as her husband. He talked about this wonderful woman he had been married to; how life would not be the same without her. Then he spoke about their two children, a four-year-old daughter and nine-year-old son. That's when the husband broke down sobbing about the children growing up without their mother, how raising them was going to be difficult, but that he could never imagine marrying another woman. The fact they would graduate from high school, get married, and have families of their own, things she would never see. Tran suddenly started to feel his heart grow heavy. He felt a sorrowful depression and tremendous guilt. The gentleman stepped down, and then a woman went to the podium. She introduced herself as the victim's younger sister, Anna. She talked about her older sister who always looked out for her. Heather was the best sister she could ever have. Heather was her best friend and whenever she needed someone to talk to she could always go to her sister. She could call her any day, any night, any time. Now she couldn't imagine how life would be without her. Anna got angry and started yelling, "How could this happen?" She started to moan and tremble, weeping uncontrollably. As her face turned red and blotchy, with bloodshot eyes, and puffy eyelids, she looked out into the crowd, "It isn't fair, it just isn't fair." Friends and family sprang to her aid, giving comfort and leading her back to the pew.

Tran couldn't take it anymore. He got up and ran out of the church. An undercover cop saw him and followed. When Tran got outside, he started crying loudly. When the officer witnessed how upset Tran was, the idea he could be a cold-blooded murderer was quickly dismissed. The profile of the Cat Scratch Killer they had come up with did not match Tran's behavior.

Chapter 7 - Obsession

For the next few days, Tran kept to himself. Talina was growing more and more concerned. Tran told her that he felt like he was coming down with something, so he spent most of his time in his room. He tried to sleep as much as he could. Otherwise, he would be consumed with thoughts of the victim. Everything raced through his mind. The actual kill, comments from other people at the funeral, the fact that she had children and a loving husband, a sister who saw her as a best friend, and several friends and family who showed up at her funeral. This is something that a killer does not get involved with. *So why did I go to this woman's funeral?* Since he had feelings for Talina, if anything happened to her he could picture himself going to her funeral. Then he imagined someone doing the same thing to her. All kinds of different emotions filled inside of him as he pictured someone killing her. Now he had an idea of how this woman's husband felt. He also had a feeling of how her sister felt. Tran saw Talina as his best friend, how lonely it was before he met Talina. He remembered how much hate he had in his heart and how much loneliness filled inside of him at the time. Would this be enough to stop him from killing in the future?

By the third day, Tran had to go back to work. Thoughts came to mind on how to leave more stalking messages for Talina to get more attention. It was easy for him to think about all this while he was working. With the kind of job he had, he could daydream all day. After a week had passed by, it seemed like a distant memory. On Saturday morning, Tran came out of his room and was watching TV. Talina slept until around 10am. She got up to find Tran watching television in the living room.

"Hey, what's going on with you?" Talina asked Tran.

"Nothing much. What do you have planned for the day?"

"I'm just going to take it easy today. Then, I have an eight hour shift tonight for overtime," Talina told Tran. "The hospital is giving away some extra shifts on the weekend. The pay is pretty good. The hospital pays extra for weekends and night shifts. Since this was overtime, I'll get paid time and a half."

Tran felt let down. He looked forward to the weekends when Talina would be home. "Well, I'm disappointed that you have to work tonight. I was hoping we could do something. Maybe we can catch a matinee tomorrow."

"Yeah, I'm sorry we can't do anything tonight. I'm not going to make this a habit. I just thought I could earn a little extra money, and I wasn't sure if you were still sick. If I'm not too tired tomorrow, the matinee sounds like fun," Talina agreed.

*****

Later that day, Talina went to work while Tran rested on the couch. He thought back to when he was a teenager, homeless and living in Fort Myers, Florida. It was not easy for Tran after his grandmother died. Hanging out with Chloe, Jamaal and Randy who were homeless just like him. They became his best friends. He would often get in fights with other kids just to steal their money to score pot, speed, or acid. Sometimes his friends shared their stash with him. But most of the money he got his hands went to buy food. For the most part, he hated girls, but Chloe was different. She was more of a tomboy. On more than one occasion, she could've ratted him out, but she didn't. She always had his back. That's how he knew he could trust her. She gained the respect of the streets and didn't need anyone to fight for her. She was tough like a guy that way, standing on her own. Tran told Chloe the story about his mother abusing him, but he never told her that he killed her. Others would tease him about never having a girlfriend and suspected he was gay. She would stand up for him and tell others that he just didn't care for most girls because of the abuse he had from his mother. She was quick to tell others that he was not gay. Later in life, he could get an erection just by watching a woman's eyes while he strangled her. It sexually excited him.

One time another homeless girl named Roe came on to him. He kept telling her to get away from him, but she would not listen. She wanted to have sex. Finally, he slammed her against the wall in the alley, then threw her on the ground and got on top of her. He wrapped his hands around her neck, trying to strangle her. She was coughing and struggling to get away. Right before she passed out, he let go of his grip. "That's what you get. You stupid bitch! I told you to leave me alone." Tran yelled at her as he walked away, leaving her lying on the ground. He wanted to kill her but didn't want to gain a reputation for murdering homeless teenagers. Then nobody would want to be his friend. His hatred towards women grew ten times deeper that day.

It was late one night when Tran committed a crime with his friends that made him leave Fort Myers. Tran, Chloe, Jamal and Randy decided to hit a local convenience store. The plan went wrong when Randy jumped over the counter and started stabbing the clerk for no reason. The clerk had already given all the money from the register to Jamal. They had all agreed earlier that no one was to get hurt. Hurting the clerk would raise the stakes for all of them. Everyone bolted on foot from the scene. Tran knew he needed to leave town before the police figured out who was there during the stabbing. He fled to a local train yard. One of the trains was moving north. Jumping on an empty car, he knew he would never see his friends again since Randy probably killed the clerk. Tran wasn't about to pay for someone else's stupid mistake. The sound of the cars rocking on the rails kept him company until he fell asleep. When he awoke in the morning, he found himself nearing Atlanta. As the train slowed down, Tran jumped off. A local diner's neon sign was visible from the train yard. In their dumpster, he found some half-eaten pancakes and a piece of bacon. With his fingers, he shoveled the food down quickly since he hadn't eaten in two days. Nearby, the bathroom of a local fast food restaurant seemed a good place to wash up. Then he headed back to the train yard. From there he thought to continue northwest.

While he hid behind some train cars, he could see the train he was on earlier start moving. It was going in the same direction, so he jumped on a different boxcar. This one had St. Louis painted in bright letters on the side of it.

Tran never felt more alone than he did at that moment. He had a new start in life, but this would not be easy for him. There was no family and nobody to care for him; no one to make him feel safe. As the train made its way west, and with nothing to do, Tran fell into a troubled asleep which consisted of several childhood nightmares. The train would make a few stops but they were quick. When it pulled into a St. Louis train yard, he hopped off and went to scavenge something to eat. As he searched the dumpsters behind restaurants, he ran into a kid who was a couple years younger. Josh was 12 years old and new to the streets. His father had recently died and his mother became an alcoholic. He ran away from home because he couldn't handle watching his mother throw her life away. Since Tran knew a little bit about living on the streets he took Josh under his wing. It didn't take long for the two of them to become friends. Josh could see that there was a dark side to Tran and quickly learned to leave him alone whenever he was in one of his moods. One day Josh saw another side of Tran that he never wanted to see again. There were a couple girls hanging out at the local arcade. Josh wanted to meet them but Tran didn't so he left and went back to their hangout, which was a large box in an alley. The next thing he knew Josh brought the two girls back to their hangout. Tran got so enraged and started violently shoving one of the girls and screaming for them to get out while yelling at Josh. The girls ran off and Josh stood there scared. The sinister tone of Tran's voice was frightening. Tran could have seriously hurt him. He apologized to Tran and left so that Tran could cool down. He returned a couple hours later to see if Tran was all right. Things seemed to be fine, but Josh never knew that Tran had such hatred for women. Josh hung out with Tran for the next two years until social services found him. They sent him to a foster home. That's when Tran began killing women.

*****

Cat Scratch Killer

When Talina's shift ended at midnight, she went to her car. She noticed the bloodied body of a rat nearby on the ground. As she approached the driver's side of her car, Talina saw the words "I see you!" written in blood. At first, she thought she was going to be sick. Shocked and scared, she ran back into the hospital screaming. The front desk person dialed 911 and gave the phone to her. After filing a report with the on-duty officer at the St. Louis Police Department, she then called a couple of co-workers who weren't working that night to tell them what happened. They told her they were coming to the hospital, insisting she go out for drinks with them. Still reeling from seeing her car vandalized, she finally agreed.

As far as Tran knew, Talina's shift was supposed to end at midnight. She had not come home yet. As the night progressed, he grew angrier and angrier at her. It was 2am and he was starting to think he should go out and look for her himself. He started pacing the apartment and talking to himself. *Where could she be and why hasn't she come home yet?* Curiously, he couldn't wait to hear her version of the stalker message he left on her car door.

She stumbled in around 2:30am, and she was drunk.

When Tran saw her, he was pissed. "Where have you been? I have been worried about you. You're drunk, aren't you?" Tran said as he raised his voice at Talina. "This isn't like you, Talina.

You don't drink much alcohol. In fact, you don't even keep any around the apartment."

"Well, excuse me for having fun. Maybe I wanted to get out and have fun with my other friends. You know you're not the only friend I have in this world!" Talina slurred in a sarcastic drunk voice. Then she staggered off to her room and slammed the door. This time she didn't mention a word about her stalker or the message on the car to Tran.

"Fine! You need to sleep it off anyway!" Tran yelled as he stormed to his room and slammed his door, too. He turned on his music so he wouldn't have to listen to hers. It didn't matter anyway since she was passed out on her bed. He lay wake most of the night upset with her. This time Tran didn't want to go out and hurt anyone. He was afraid to leave the apartment in case Talina came out and hurt herself.

Finally at about 4:30am, he dozed off. It was a little after 10 Sunday morning when Talina came out to watch TV. She watched the news. Soon after, Tran woke up, Hearing the television, he came out of his room and sat on the couch next to her. Neither one of them said anything for a while.

When a commercial came on, Tran looked at Talina, "You were pretty drunk last night."

Talina looked at him with a dopey smirk, "I was? I don't remember coming home. I went out with a couple friends after work. They've wanted me to go out with them for a while now. I kept turning them down. I guess I should have told you, but I forgot to call you. I'm sorry."

Tran wondered why she didn't say anything about the message on her car. He got up and walked to the kitchen, then turned around, "Well, next time you need to call and let me know. I was so worried about you. Don't you ever do that to me again!" Changing the subject, he asked, "How was your shift last night?"

"Fine. Everything was fine," she replied. Talina decided not to tell him that she spoke to the police. She reasoned since he had been against it before, he would be against it this time too.

Later that day, he checked her car to only see that it had been washed. He was very disappointed when he saw his handiwork was not having the desired effect. Tran wanted to hate her like he did with all women. He was filled with anger but conflicted with love at the same time. Talina would be dead by now if it weren't for the feelings that Tran had for her.

She got up and joined him in the kitchen "You're right. I'll call next time. I'm sorry. I should know better." Since Talina had a hangover, the two of them stayed home and found a movie on TV to watch. They made microwave popcorn along with other snacks while the movie played.

Talina had to go to work on Monday, but Tran was off. Little by little he started going through her private things while she was at work. She had a box in her closet, full of personal items. These were items from her school years. He discovered a prom picture with a good-looking guy. She was undeniably beautiful in the picture, wearing a gorgeous long royal blue dress. He decided to keep this picture for himself. Then he looked through other pictures with her friends but there were hardly any pictures with guys. Why didn't she have pictures with boyfriends? Or love letters? This was odd since he distinctly remembered Talina talking about a boyfriend in high school. Her parents were still living, so he assumed that she had left those things at their house. He also found some pictures of Jasmine. It looked like pictures of them in nursing school. You could tell they were good friends. She didn't talk much about Jasmine. Maybe it was too painful for her. He found another good picture of her that someone had taken. He decided to keep this picture as well as the prom picture. Tran tried to make it look the same as before, placing the box back in her closet. His curiosity got the better of him so he went through her dresser to see if he could find anything else. He wanted to cut the guy out of the photo, but he knew that if she ever asked about the picture, he would have to sneak it back into the box. He would have to make sure the picture was not damaged. Tran took the two pictures to his room.

It was about 11am when the phone rang. Tran answered and it was a guy asking for Talina. Tran told him that she was at work. He asked if he could take the message. He pretended to look for some paper and a pen. The guy said he was a friend from an old job she worked with. After he hung up the phone, he paced around the apartment for several minutes. *She's keeping in touch with guys? I'm the only guy in her life now!* Enraged, he wanted to break things, hurt someone, or hurt himself. He didn't know what to do. He went into his room and tore off the top sheet and started ripping it to shreds with his fingers until it was in small, tiny pieces. By the time he was done he was exhausted. Then he just started crying. He didn't understand the feelings of sadness and crying anymore. He did that as a child and it didn't get him any sympathy, especially from his mother. Usually he would be angry, but this time he cried for so long that he fell asleep. The sound of the front door unlocking woke him up. Talina was coming home from work. He quickly came out of his room, shutting his door behind him so that she would not see the bedsheet torn to shreds all over his floor and ask questions. She could never know the rage that was inside of him. As she came in, he was coming down the hall into the living room.

"Hey, Talina, how was work?" Tran innocently asked as he turned on the TV, still feeling the fury inside.

"It was busy. They got a lot of new admits over the week-end." Talina answered on the way to her bedroom.

While Talina changed, Tran made dinner, so she wouldn't have to cook. He made hot dogs, macaroni and cheese. She was in a much better mood.

"So, what did you do all day?" Talina asked.

Tran resented having to make small talk just to avoid exploding about discovering that other guys rang her phone. "Well I'll be honest, I pretty much did nothing. I watched TV most of the day. I have a long workday tomorrow and the weather is supposed to be hot so I decided to just take it easy today."

Talina smiled, "Oh, that's right. It's supposed to be in the upper 90's tomorrow. You need to be careful. You don't want to have a heat stroke while doing all that yard work. Make sure you drink plenty of liquids." Talina said as she took her plate back to the kitchen. She washed up the dinner dishes, and went back into the living room to watch a little TV with Tran before going to bed. Tran wished that she stayed up later, but he understood that she had to get up early the next morning to be at work by 7am.

The next morning, Tran got up about the same time that Talina did. The more yard work he and his coworkers got done in the early morning, the less they would have to do in the afternoon when it was the hottest. They finished around 4pm. It was a good thing because the thermometer showed temps of almost 99°. It felt good to come home and take a nice cool shower. He collapsed on the couch with the TV on and fell asleep, he was so exhausted.

Talina came home around 7:30pm again. Neither one of them felt like cooking, so dinner was whatever each of them could find in the refrigerator.

Tran hated it when Talina was doing her four-day work run. She didn't get to spend much time with him so he felt lonely. His behavior started to get even stranger. One time he left a pair of store bought ladies panties hanging on her car antenna. They looked very similar to her choice of underwear she had at home. He always left unsettling gifts on her car while it was parked at her work. This led police to believe the stalker was someone from the hospital or a past patient. Lately, he started going into Talina's bedroom and watching her sleep. He would stand on whichever side she was facing, watch her sleep for about 20 minutes, and then go back to his room. She woke up one night and swore she saw him in her room.

The next morning she confronted him, "Tran, were you in my room last night?

"No. Why would you think that?"

That's when she was sure that it was just a dream. After she challenged him about that, he refrained from doing it for a while. He didn't want to get caught because this could cause real problems in the relationship.

One day while she was at work, he went to her room and took out a pair of her panties from the dirty clothes. They still had her scent on them. With his eyes closed, he held them up to his face and took a deep breath in through his nose. He imagined himself with her at that moment. He continued to do this for several minutes. Then he walked to his room, taking the panties with him. These were his panties now. Any time he wanted to imagine her around, he would close his eyes and sniff her emerald green satin black lace panties. He had to keep these in a safe place where she would not find them, under his mattress at the head of his bed.

*****

That night, Tran would have a nightmare he had every once in a while. When Tran was a baby his mother, Jackie, would hold him underwater and scream at him to stop crying. She would do this because she couldn't stand the loud noise. She didn't know that he had colic. This angered her so much that she would take him to the kitchen, fill the sink up with water, and then hold his face down into the water to get him to stop crying. The only reason he stopped crying was because he would pass out. He was about six months old when she did this to him. She hated having a child. He was nothing but a nuisance for her. When he was a toddler, he would often get earaches. The pain was so bad that he would rock himself to sleep. If he cried it would only make her angry. The earaches happened so often, the rocking became a habit. This habit would follow him into adulthood. He had partial hearing loss in his left ear because one of the infections got really bad and was left untreated. When he would have nightmares like this, he would wake up with a lot of anger.

Usually, Talina was already gone for work so he wouldn't vent his anger on her. On days when she was off, and Tran woke up full of anger, he would get up, get dressed, and go out for a long walk to calm down before coming back home.

Often, when Talina would get home from work, she would be exhausted. Incidents kept occurring at work causing untold stress and restless sleep for her. She would go to Tran for comfort but not tell him of the police involvement. Talina began to have nightmares and exhibit paranoia since the police couldn't seem to catch this guy.

One particular Friday evening she just wanted to stay home and watch TV. Tran wanted to watch TV with her, but had an idea. He volunteered to go down to the local video store to rent a movie that they could both watch. While Tran stepped out, Talina decided to make a simple dinner for both of them. Tran had a short walk to the video store. As he was walking, it was almost dark. The thought entered his mind to find a victim and do another killing. But the anticipation of getting to spend some quality time with Talina quickly entered his mind. He picked up his stride as this pleasantly engulfed his thoughts. As he got to the video store, he wondered what she would like to watch. He imagined watching a love drama with her. This caused him to head to the drama section of the store. As he combed through the many movies available, he found a love romance story about a child looking for a woman to fall in love with his single father. This movie had two big actors that played the leading roles. The whole time he was in the rental store, he kept his head down so as to not be recognized. When he took the movie up to the register, he continued to hold his head down, acting like he had a stutter as he spoke. As he left the video store, he quickly walked back to the apartment. As he walked in, he realized that Talina had made hamburgers, macaroni and cheese. Without telling her what movie he got, he put the movie in the VCR and pushed play. Talina brought his dinner to him and gave him a soda. She went back to the kitchen to get herself a drink and her dinner. Then she joined him on the couch. As the movie began, Tran expressed how excited he was to get to watch the movie with her. He hoped that by Talina watching the movie, she might have romantic thoughts towards him. As the movie got deeper into the story, Talina started to feel a little uncomfortable. Suddenly, she grabbed a handful of nuts that she had sat out earlier and one by one started throwing them at Tran. She was in a playful mood. At first, he wasn't sure why she was doing this, but he then realized she wanted him to play along. They started laughing and having a good time. In a playful way, Talina lightly started smacking his face. He did the same to her and before they knew it, they were on the floor wrestling.

Then, Talina stopped and laid there just laughing. "Oh my God, that was too much fun. I haven't laughed this hard in a long time," Talina said as she tried to slow her breathing down.

"You know, this has been the most fun I've had in a long time as well. So, do you think we can get back to the movie?" Tran asked with a smile on his face.

"Well, if you insist bonehead!" Talina responded with a little laugh. They got up off the floor, sat back on the couch and continued to watch the movie. Tran was disappointed that this was the only time they interacted that night. When the movie ended, Talina got up and thanked Tran for a fun night. She went to her room and soon after, went to bed. Tran picked up the peanuts off the floor, cleaned the small amount of dishes and went to his room. At first, he felt sad that Talina did not give him more attention, but then he realized that she was the one who instigated playing around. This made him think that this could be the beginning of her becoming interested in him. Maybe the movie he chose was a success.

When Sunday came, Tran and Talina decided to go to Kirkwood and hang out near the Amtrak station where there was outdoor seating for lunch. It was across from the courthouse in downtown Kirkwood. It was a beautiful sunny day in the low 90s.

They had fun talking and watching people. Talina enjoyed looking at a couple of guys she thought were cute. She didn't tell Tran, because she started realizing that he had a little crush on her. But Tran had a more sinister thought in mind. This was an area where he had killed a young woman.

*****

One particular night, he had taken the city bus and was dropped off in this area of Kirkwood. He sat in one of the chairs in this outdoor seating area, contemplating a kill so he had his gym bag with him. It was early evening and the chairs had not been locked up yet. He noticed a young petite girl with long brown hair. She was walking alone. He got up and started following her, realizing that she was walking to her car. He sped up faster to get to her before she could get inside her car and lock the doors. As she opened her car door, he grabbed her hair with his left hand and jerked her back. He put his right hand over her mouth. Then he whispered in her ear to open the car door to the back seat. As she opened the door, he kicked the front driver's door shut. He shoved her into the back seat and jumped on top of her, shutting the car door behind him. Tran sat on top of her and put both his hands around her throat, squeezing as hard as he could. She was trying to scream, but she couldn't get a sound out. Tears started streaming down her face as she knew that she was about to die. She fought as hard as she could. With a little bit of light shining though from the building next door Tran could see her eyes. He stared into her eyes as he could feel her body go limp. He continued to hold his grip to make sure that she was dead. Then he slowly released. Taking a deep breath, he looked around to make sure that no one could see him. Then he looked back down at his victim and could see her eyes, the life gone from them. He could see the marks around her throat where he had his grip. He grabbed his gym bag that had fallen to the floor of the car. He pulled out the back scratcher, the Walkman, and his earbuds initiating the ritual he did for all his victims.

Chapter 8 – The Warehouse

Talina knew Tran didn't have a camera to take pictures so she decided to get him a really nice camera for Christmas. When Tran opened up the Christmas present, he was elated. Over the next couple months, he took several pictures of Talina. In fact, he was obsessed with taking pictures of her with or without her consent. He would fill up his camera with pictures then take it to the local Wal-Mart and have prints made. He hung them on the wall in his closet. The clothes covered the pictures so that Talina would not discover them.

Tran craved the smell of Talina. He went into her room one night with a pair of scissors and slowly walked to the side of her bed. With her back towards him, he took snippets of her hair. Then he slowly walked out of her room, being ever so careful not to get caught. Tran went to the kitchen and put the locks of hair in a small plastic bag. He took the baggie back to his room and put it with the rest of the mementos he collected from Talina in a small wooden box. The next day after she had gone to work, he took some of her shampoo and her shower gel, putting them in containers so he would have the scent of her with him always. As the months went by, he continued to do odd things to be closer to Talina.

One day Talina came home from work and asked Tran if he wanted to go on road trip. She had an idea to drive to Branson, Missouri for her birthday. She had three days off and she wanted to take an extra day off so that she would have four days off in a row. Tran would have to ask his boss for time off. Since it was fall, the lawn business was slowing down. He thought this was a great idea. He called his boss and he was able to get off but it would mean that he would have to work this weekend. Tran wasn't sure how he was going to afford it but Talina insisted on paying for everything.

Before they knew, it was time for the trip. They packed everything in her small little car, bought snacks and got on the road. They took Highway 44 W. It was about 5am on Friday morning. Since it was still dark outside, there wasn't much traffic yet. They were both coffee drinkers so they stopped by at a local gas station and filled up the gas tank, getting coffee for the road.

"This is going to be a lot of fun. I'm glad you thought of this," Tran grinned.

Talina sipped her coffee. "Yep, I know we'll have a lot of fun. I think we needed this."

As they got on the road, it didn't take long before the sun came up. The sky was clear and beautiful. Every half an hour they took turns listing to their favorite music. Talina liked country music, especially Shania Twain and Tran liked rock 'n roll. Every so often, they would stop for a bathroom break. When they finally arrived in Branson Talina remarked that it looked a lot like pictures of Vegas. Everything was so fancy. There was so much to see that it was hard to decide what to do first. They decided to go to the Visitors Bureau to find out what attractions were available. Picking up some brochures, they checked into a local motel. The Baldknobbers and the Presleys shows seemed like fun since they were staying in Branson for a couple days. Tran couldn't remember the last time he had so much fun. He laughed so hard during the Baldknobber Show, he thought his stomach was going to split open. Talina was so happy to see him laughing. This was a rare occasion. They were sitting in the third row right in the middle. It was beautiful theater seating.

When the show was over, they strolled out in the parking lot. A guy leered at Talina, "Hey, you look hot in that dress!"

Tran got so upset, that he punched him in the face. When he fell to the ground, Tran quickly jumped on top of him, rabbit punching him over and over again. Blood started streaming from the man's nose, and mouth. People started gathering around. Talina was screaming for him to stop. After about 20 blows, Tran finally stopped. The man was not moving and his face was covered in blood. Talina just stood there in shock. She could not believe that Tran could do such a thing to another human being. She couldn't understand the rage that came out of him just because some stranger made a comment about her. The man didn't even harm her. What else was he capable of? Everyone just stood there in silence. Tran looked up and saw people staring at him. He slowly stood up, turned around and looked at Talina. He realized that he would not be able to explain this to her. He walked past her to the passenger side of her car, waiting for her to unlock the car doors. Talina quickly realized that they had better leave before the police got there. As the bystanders called the police, they drove straight to their motel and checked out, driving back east on Highway 44. Talina was so angry at Tran she told him to lay down in the back seat for most of the trip home in case the police spotted them. After they passed Rolla, she told him he could sit back up. She would need time to digest what she had seen. Tran knew he really screwed up this time. He couldn't believe that for most of the trip, they had so much fun and now they were going home with so much misery.

"I'm sorry I lost it back there. That guy disrespected you. I was only trying to protect you." Tran tried to apologize to her but Talina didn't care to listen to him.

She waited for a moment, and then took a deep breath. "You went way too far. You tried to kill that man. Hitting him once or twice is one thing but hitting him over and over again was insane. What were you thinking? All I could see was rage coming from you."

Tran was silent for a moment as he tried to think of an answer to give her. "When I was young I saw a lot of violence with adults. As a teenager I lived on the streets and saw a lot of violence. Most of the time, that's how I survived. Living with you I am learning that I don't need to do that. But it's taking time. I'm sorry you had to see that today. I have become a better person because of you and I thank you."

Both of them were quiet for a few minutes.

Then, Talina spoke, "You have got to promise me that you will never do that again. I mean it Tran. Promise me!"

Tran looked at her. "All right, all right, I get it!"

At that moment they both found the song that they could listen to, however, neither one felt like singing. They never brought the subject of that day up again.

Deep inside Tran was still agitated. He had built up rage that needed to be unleashed. As Talina continued to drive, Tran thought about killing. He was trying to think of an excuse to use her car once they returned to her apartment. Maybe he could tell her they needed groceries or tell her he just needed think for a while. Or maybe just make up something like visiting a friend from work. That would be better. That way he wouldn't have to worry about bringing home anything afterwards.

As they got closer to home, Talina tried to make small talk. Tran knew that she wasn't mad at him anymore, but it didn't make him feel any better. She had already seen a part of him that he had been trying so hard to hide. This was a major setback for him. The thought of this made him more agitated. He needed to release this anger. He knew he couldn't stay home with Talina tonight. He had already made the decision to kill.

When they arrived at her apartment, Talina went in and made them dinner. She warmed up some leftover spaghetti that was in the fridge. It was going on 7:30pm and getting dark.

After dinner, Tran nonchalantly asked, "Hey, is it ok if I borrow your car and go see a friend from work? I just need to get out for a while."

"Sure, do you know how late you will be?"

"No, but I shouldn't be too late."

Tran answered as he got up and walked to his room. He grabbed his gym bag and sat it next to the front door.

"Boy, you never go anywhere without that bag, do you?" Talina said jokingly.

Tran quickly looked at her and smiled. He realized he better not look suspicious about it. "Thanks for the car. I'll see you later." He grabbed his bag and stepped out, pulling the door shut behind him. At once his demeanor changed. With no expression on his face, he walked to the car. He slowly unlocked it and sat inside. As he pulled the driver's door shut, he stared forward as if he were hypnotized. After a couple minutes, he started the engine. He slowly drove the streets, looking for his next victim. The car radio was off, leaving only his thoughts to play in his mind. His feelings were mixed. He had the anger inside but yet he could hear Talina's voice telling him to be a good person. This confused him as well as irritated him.

Suddenly, there she was. His next victim was crossing the street. He sat at the stoplight and watched her. She continued down the sidewalk. As the light changed, the driver behind him grew impatient and honked his horn. It caught the girl's attention as she looked back at the cars stopped at the light. Tran pulled forward and parked the car. The girl continued to walk. He quickly got out and started following her, picking up the pace to close the distance between them. He noticed she was walking to an area that was not well lit. As he caught up with her, he placed his hand on her right shoulder.

"Ma'am, I think you dropped these," Tran said as he held out his car keys.

"No, those are not mine," she answered.

He looked around to make sure nobody was watching, and then placed his right hand on her mouth. He wrapped his left arm around the front of her waist, picked her up and carried her to the side of a nearby building. She kicked her legs trying to free herself. He threw her down on the ground and jumped on top of her. Placing both hands on her throat, he squeezed as hard as he could. She continued to kick and fight. As he kept squeezing, he heard Talina's soft voice, her laughter, her smile. This kill was different. He looked at this girl's eyes and they looked a lot like Talina's. Tran started having a moral conscious about this killing. A tear started rolling out of his left eye. He felt his heart pounding harder and feeling heavy. Everything was wrong about this. He started to let go of his grip but the girl had already passed out. He slowly let go of his grip, and climbed off her body. He was out of breath. He looked around realizing that he forgot his bag in the car. It didn't matter. She was still alive. What would he do now? He couldn't leave her there. When she awoke, she would go to the police and identify him. He needed to take her somewhere until he could figure out what to do with her. He jumped up to his feet and ran to the car. He pulled up close the building, got out and dragged her body to the car. He put her in the front passenger seat so he could keep an eye on her if she came to.

He drove around for about ten minutes when an idea came to him. There was an old abandoned warehouse about eight minutes away. His victim started waking up before they got to the warehouse. He grabbed her hair so she wouldn't try to flee from the car while he was driving.

"What is your name?" Tran asked her.

"Kristy," she cried.

"Kristy, if you do what I tell you, I will not kill you." Tran pulled the car around to the back of the warehouse. Since it was dark outside, the beam from the headlights faced the building. He pulled her out through his driver's side. She continued to cry as he forced her to walk inside.

"Why are you bringing me here?" she pleaded.

Tran didn't say anything as he continued to walk her into the building. He found an area on the second level and told her to kneel on the floor. This time he had his bag with him. He needed something to tie her up with so he got out a shirt from the bag. He tore it to shreds and used it to bind her hands and feet. Then, he knelt down.

"Kristy, I'm sorry I did this to you. I wanted to kill you earlier, but I couldn't. Someone has changed me. I just don't know if I can let you go. I mean, the minute I let you go, you will go to the police," Tran explained.

"No, I won't. Please, just let me go," she pleaded as tears rolled down her face. She had the gut feeling that she was with the killer that had been in the news. Terrified that she would be the next victim to be found, she remembered how they were found. She wondered if he would put marks across her back. She was sure she would never see her family again. She had a sister seven years younger than herself. She knew she would never see her boyfriend again. She had hoped to marry him someday.

Tran laced his fingers behind his head and paced the floor in front of his victim. He wasn't sure what to do. He decided to tell her everything so that someone could tell the police and media his story in case something should happen to him before he could explain to Talina. She was the one person he wanted to understand him. He was in a panic to get back home, knowing Talina would wonder.

"I need to leave, but I will be back in the morning. I need to tell you things before I can let you go. Please understand that I have to do this first. Then you will go home." Tran explained.

He used part of his shirt to tie her to a pole so she could not leave the building. He tied another part of his shirt around her face to cover her mouth so she could not be heard if she tried to scream. Then Tran went back to the car and drove back to the apartment.

He thought about leaving his victim in the dark. It was about 10:20pm when he walked in the door. Talina had already gone to bed since she had to go to work the next day. Tran had to go to work too but he decided that he would call in sick. He wasn't sure how he would get to the warehouse without a car. It was about a fifteen minute drive from their apartment. Maybe a city bus would work. It was a sleepless night for Tran. His brain kept running images of his victim escaping and going to the police before he could convince her that he was not a bad person.

Back at the warehouse, Kristy was able to lie sideways on the cold hard cement. It was dark with no light in the room. The sound of rats and other rodents crawling through the building made her cringe. She felt a bite on her ankle and screamed thru the shirt that covered her mouth. She tried to kick but it was difficult with both legs tied. Kristy started trembling. Her imagination heightened all of her senses. By morning, she was exhausted with fear.

Tran took a bus as far as he could go, but still had to walk a long way. When he got to the warehouse, he went up to the second level to find Kristy curled up in a fetal position. Her eyes were open but she was not responsive. She looked like she was in shock. He removed the gag from her mouth.

"Hey Kristy! Can you hear me? Kristy! Kristy!" Tran said in a stern voice.

Slowly, her eyes looked up at him and started to tear up.

"Hey, you're ok. I'm back. Here, I'm going to sit you up."

Tran untied her hands from the pole then retied them together. "Are you hungry?" he asked as he opened his bag.

"I need to go to the bathroom." she replied in a soft voice.

He thought for a minute, looked around. "Do you just need to pee?" Tran asked.

She nodded her head yes.

"OK, I'm going to take you to that corner over there, pull your pants down enough for you to go to bathroom, then you are going to squat and pee. OK?" Tran explained.

She nodded her head. He helped her stand up and walked her over to the other side of the room. As he pulled her pants down, she started crying with embarrassment. He tried to calm her down by talking about his feelings for Talina. It did seem to calm her down a little when she realized that he was not focused on her sexually. When she finished, he pulled her pants back up. He took her back to the corner they were when he was about to give her something to eat. He had brought a sandwich and water for her. As she sat down, he handed her the bottled water first after taking the cap off.

"Please, drink some water. I don't want you getting dehydrated. Think about it, Kristy. If I was planning on killing you, why would I give you something to eat and drink? It's because I am not going to kill you. But I do need for you to understand some things before I let you go." Tran said as he handed her the sandwich.

There was no other way to handle this. He really didn't want to kill her. Talina had changed him. He realized that now. He had to let his victim go but he didn't know what would happen to him. How would he have a relationship with Talina now? This victim is sure to go to the police. The only thing he thought he could do is to tell Talina the truth and hope that she would care enough to protect him. As all these thoughts came to him, he realized that Talina couldn't find this out from the police or from the media. It must be from him or she would not really understand.

Tran sat on the floor in front of his victim and told her about his childhood. It didn't take long for Kristy to calm down and realize that he was talking to her like a person, not his victim. She wasn't sure what to think of this but started to understand the chaos in his life. Over the next couple hours, she started interacting with him in conversation. Then he started talking about his killings. She grew silent as he described why and how he started killing. He didn't feel the need to go over all the killings but wanted her to understand why he let this behavior ruin his life. He told her that now he wished he had never done these acts, that meeting Talina had changed him. Kristy found this interesting. It occurred to her that she might live through this because of Talina.

So she decided to focus on her and got Tran to talk about her. He felt at ease with Kristy when talking about Talina. This was the first time he had been able to talk to anyone about how he felt about Talina. Before they both knew it, they had been talking for hours. For the first time in Tran's life, everything made sense. Everything had meaning. He had purpose and now he didn't need to kill. This was a breakthrough for him.

Kristy felt torn. She started having empathy for Tran and second guessing about the need to go to the police. She asked herself if he could actually change. After all, he could have killed her last night.

Tran stood up and paced the floor. "I need to let you go now. I'm taking a big chance that you will go to the police but that's the chance I have to take. I can't kill you. That's not me anymore. Your freedom is more important." Tran said as he took the ties off her hands and feet.

Kristy didn't say anything.

"I'm going to leave. Wait about ten minutes, then you can go. Kristy, I'm sorry I put you though this." Tran apologized, then left the building. When Tran got outside, he ran where she would not see which direction he took. He practically sprinted all the way back to Talina's apartment.

As Kristy waited, she thought about everything Tran had shared with her. She kept running all the abuse through her mind that his mother subjected him to. She was tormented by how normal he seemed to be with her. He spoke to her as if he knew her for years. She actually started to feel comfortable with him. How could this man be the same persona, the monster who wanted to kill her the night before? Realizing that the ten minutes must have passed by, she stood up and approached the stairs. Kristy made her way slowly down the stairs and walked outside. There was still about an hour of daylight left. As she continued to walk past various storefronts on the street, she pondered over going to the police.

Chapter 9 – The Last Kill

Tran got home, immediately went to his room, and shut the door. He sat on the bed, leaning his back against the wall, staring straight ahead, just thinking. Life was about to change but he wasn't exactly sure how. It was only a matter of time before Kristy would go to the police. *Why did I tell her so much? Maybe I should have left her there and skipped town, then called the police to report where she could be found. No, I'd never be able to see Talina again if I did that. I need to tell Talina everything, except about Jasmine. She would never forgive me for killing her. But first I need to think about what to do if the police come after me. I can't let them take me alive. I need a gun.*

Tran still had some contacts on the streets. Grabbing his gym bag, he ran out of the apartment to the nearby bus stop. He saw some people waiting and asked if they knew what buses would take him to downtown St. Louis. One guy seemed to know a lot about the bus schedules. Lewis wrote the information down quickly, and then boarded the next bus. But Tran had to wait another thirty minutes for his bus. Waiting took forever. His eyes kept darting around nervously to make sure there were no police. He followed Lewis's advice and took the buses needed to make it downtown. Finally, the bus was in a familiar part of town and he could start looking for JJ. JJ was the one you went to if you needed a weapon that was not registered. He owed Tran a favor since helping him evade police after they thought he killed another homeless kid. Later, police learned that JJ did not kill him. After inquiring around, he was able to find JJ in an abandoned house.

"Tran, my man! Where have you been? I thought you had left this earth, man," JJ said as he welcomed Tran in.

"Nope, I'm alive and well, dude. I need to talk to you though. It's important."

Yeah, sure man."

JJ eyeballed three other people in the room and they walked out.

"JJ, I got myself into some serious shit. The heat is looking for me. I need a piece. I won't let them take me alive," Tran pleaded.

"Yeah, man. Hold on." He walked out of the room. A few minutes later JJ returned with a Beretta in his hand. "Here. I'm not going to ask what you did. I just need you to leave and don't come back. I don't need the cops here. You watch yourself Tran."

Tran took the gun and stuck it into his gym bag. "Thanks, man. I knew I could count on you." It was time to get out of this side of town because not everyone liked him there and to get back before Talina wondered what happened to him.

Sure enough as Tran arrived, Talina was taking a pizza out of the oven. "Hey Tran, you're just in time. Want to share a pizza with me?"

"Sure, let me put my bag in my room first." Tran replied. Tran walked into his room, shut the door. He took the gun out of his bag and put it under his pillow. Then, he left his room and joined Talina for dinner and TV. He was surprised that she didn't ask where he had been since he always got home from work before she did. But Talina was so tired that she didn't even think about it. They watched some funny sitcoms and then she went to bed.

Tran wanted to watch the news to see if his victim, Kristy, had gone to the police. He watched the local news but there were no reports of her abduction. Tran began to think that maybe he convinced her not to report him to the police. He couldn't believe his good luck. There might still be a chance that she could change her mind or maybe the police just hadn't found him yet. He was exhausted, so he shut off the TV and went to bed. He didn't sleep the night before so tonight he would sleep well.

The next morning, they both had to get up for work. Talina dropped off Tran at his job. Tran had the gun with him, wrapped up in a bag with his lunch. He was prepared in case the police found him at his job, but nothing happened that day. Tran was scheduled for a long work day. Talina decided to work a half day, then pick up Tran later, if needed.

Talina was watching TV after she got home from work, when she heard a knock at the front door. She opened it to see two officers standing there.

"Hi ma'am, my name is Officer Kendrick and this is Officer Spencer. Do you have a moment where we could talk to you?" The taller officer asked.

"Sure," Talina slowly drew the words out, "Come on in." What is going on here? She led them to the kitchen table. "How can I help you?"

"We have a few questions concerning the death of your friend Jasmine," Officer Kendrick answered.

A feeling of dread suddenly came over her. She listened as Officer Spencer spoke first.

"Talina, your friend was not killed by wolves. We believe she was killed by a man we have been looking for."

"I was there. I saw the wolves tearing at her," Talina insisted.

Officer Kendrick interrupted her, "An autopsy was done, which is normal in cases of disasters. When the coroner examined the body, it was apparent that she died by strangulation." He put a photograph of Jasmine showing purple neck marks down on the table. When he examined her back, the same wounds of the Cat Scratch Killer were present."

At that moment he slammed down a photo of a different victim showing the trademark on her back. He then laid down a third photo. It showed Jasmine's back with partial scratches on her that were identical to the other photo. Talina looked back and forth at the photos. Silence filled the room. She could feel her heart pounding harder. Slowly, she formed the words, "So, are you trying to tell me that the Cat Scratch Killer from the news reports was in the mountains?" Talina asked in disbelief.

"No, I'm telling you the killer was on the train," Officer Spencer answered.

Talina's eyes widened with dread. "Are you saying that he was with us when we were rescued?"

"This is something that we need to investigate further," Officer Kendrick replied.

"Will you be available if we have any more questions Talina?" Officer Spencer asked.

"Yes, just let me know how I can help," she responded.

As the officers left, Talina slowly closed the door. She walked back over to the couch and turned the TV off. She sat and stared at the blank screen as if it would show her pictures of the past. Suddenly, she remembered the bag that Tran had. She ran to his room and got the bag from his closet. As she opened the bag she could feel her heart beating harder. She pulled out the metal back scratcher and then she pulled out a Walkman with the headsets. She put on the headsets and pushed the play button. To her horror, she listened as the music played Cat Scratch Fever. Tears rolled out from her eyes as she realized, Tran wasn't who he claimed to be. In a flash, it all made sense to her. Memories came flooding back...Tran coming back from the woods, saying that he went to the restroom...Tran not having much expression at Jasmine's death...Tran quickly saying yes to moving in with her without thinking it over first...Tran getting a job that only paid cash...Tran not keeping his money at a bank...Tran not having any credit cards or driver's license...Tran not having any other identification on him...Tran wearing his baseball cap low to his eyes in public places...Tran packing up everything he had to get on a train and go to Colorado leaving everything, even though he didn't have much...Tran never wanting to talk about his past. "Oh my God, it's him!" Talina dissolved into a heap on the bedroom floor, sobbing. Tears turned to anger as she looked for more of his stuff.

What else was hidden in his room? She started going through his drawers when she came across a pair of women's panties and some photos of her. Some photos she recognized but several were taken without her knowledge. What was most strange was that some were taken when Tran was not with her; like pictures of her coming out of work. As she took a closer look at the panties, she was shocked to see that they were hers. Then, she found a notepad that was the same paper as the notes the stalker had left for her. She realized not only was Tran The Cat Scratch Killer but her stalker as well; putting her through hell for days and weeks.

At that moment, Tran walked through the front door. "Hey Talina, it's me," Tran called out.

Talina didn't have time to discover the photos on the back wall of the closet or the wooden box full of secrets. She quickly put everything back in the drawer and closed it, then quietly ran to her room. "Hey, I'm in here." The calmness of her voice did not let Tran know that she now suspected him. She could hear him walking through the living room, entering the hallway his footsteps on the squeaky wood floor getting louder as he got closer to her door. Her heart pounded in her chest as she stared at her open doorway, knowing he was about to appear.

"Hey, how's it going?" Tran said as he greeted her.

Talina willed herself to calm down before she answered him, "Oh, I was just getting ready to look for an old school book from nursing. So how was your day, Tran?"

"It wasn't too bad. It got pretty hot today doing all that yard work." He looked at her.

Talina averted her eyes, and walked past him to the kitchen. "I need some water, how about you?"

"No, I've been sweating all day. I think I'll take a shower and then grab a Coke."

Tran went to take a shower. Talina decided a pot of coffee was needed. After it brewed, she poured herself a cup. She sat down at the kitchen table, wondering how to ask him if he was the person police were looking for without putting herself in danger. She stared at her coffee and ran her finger several times around the rim of the cup. Before she really had time to think, suddenly, the shower stopped. Her heart pounded faster. It was only a matter of time before he got dressed and came back out. Thinking about how she was going to confront the person she thought knew, her whole body started to shake, experiencing nausea, headaches, and sweating. What would she say? How would she do this by not putting him on the defensive? A couple of minutes passed. She could hear the bathroom door open and his footsteps getting closer. It would be a long night.

As Tran walked in, he could tell something was heavy on Talina's mind. "Hey, are you okay?"

Yeah, but there's something I need to talk to you about," Talina said.

Tran grabbed a Coke from the refrigerator and sat down at the table with Talina. His eyes showed concern, "So what's going on?"

"Tran, two police officers were here today." Talina started.

At that moment Tran visibly tensed up. He froze for a second, and then nonchalantly asked, "What did they say?"

"They had questions about Jasmine's death," Talina looked straight into his eyes.

"Why would they be asking about that? We told them that she died from wolves." Tran slowly said as his mind was spinning unsure of what to say next.

"She didn't die from wolves. They believe she was murdered by the Cat Scratch Killer." Talina answered as she fought back her tears. "Tran, what is going on? And don't lie to me!"

"What do you mean 'don't lie to you?'" Tran replied as his voice got louder.

Talina looked back down at her coffee and took a deep breath. She then looked directly into his eyes. She tilted her head, fighting the tears that were waiting to fall. "It's you, isn't it? Please, tell me what's going on." Talina begged.

Suddenly, Tran's demeanor changed. He was a different person. His voice went deep and sinister, "You know what's going on."

This was a side of Tran Talina had never seen before. As quickly as he changed into a dark evil person, he changed back to the Tran she knew. One minute he was one personality and another minute he was another personality. She realized that her life was in danger. But if he had lived with her all this time and did not hurt her, maybe she could reason with him? She realized that he must have feelings for her. "Tran, I don't hate you. I just need to understand. Tran, tell me!" Talina demanded.

At that moment a tear fell from Tran's right eye. His voice was back to normal as he answered. "Talina, I don't want to hurt you. I actually care about you. You are talking about a different person. I'm not that person anymore. You changed me, and I love you for that." Tran realized he would have to explain everything to Talina but if she didn't understand or if she planned to call the police, she would have to be his next victim.

If he could just take Talina to the warehouse, he would explain how he let had Kristy go. To reason with her; to prove how she had changed him. He was different person.

"I'm not going to hurt you, but I need for you to come with me. I need to show you something."

Talina was hesitant but followed him out the door anyway. As they approached her car, Tran walked over to the driver's door. "I'll drive. It's not far."

Talina stood by the car, "Tran, I don't even know if I can trust you anymore."

"I know. But just please come with me. I have to show you something good. It's important Talina," he begged

.He opened up his door and got in.

Talina did likewise on the passenger side. Tran drove her to the warehouse. Since he had not seen any news reports about Kristy's abduction and attack, he thought the warehouse would be safe.

As they pulled up, Talina got an uneasy feeling. She was confused why he would bring her to an old abandoned warehouse. "Tran, I don't think we should be here."

They both sat for a moment in silence.

Tran looked over at Talina. "It's ok. We won't be here long. Then, we can go home, and I will pack my things and leave, if that's what you want."

They both got out of the car and walked slowly towards the building. As they stepped inside, Tran took the lead. He led her to the second floor where he had kept Kristy. His dirty shirt that he used to gag Kristy's mouth was still on the floor. He walked over, picked it up and looked at Talina.

"Last night, I started to kill a woman and couldn't go through with it because of you. You changed me. For the first time, I felt bad about what I was doing. Talina, I let her go. She's alive out there somewhere. She will probably go to the police but I'm glad I decided to let her live. I don't want to kill anymore. I want a life with you. That's all I think about now. The only reason why I was out looking for a victim last night was because you and I got into a fight. I was hurt and angry. I didn't know how to process that. In the past, I would act out by finding a victim and killing them," Tran explained.

He started telling her about what happened to him as a child, hoping that would explain the person he had become. As he told her about all the trauma he went through, Talina began to cry. She couldn't imagine any child going through abuse on a daily basis. Then he started explaining the killings, but Talina couldn't handle that part.

"I don't want to hear anymore. You can't undo the things you have done. You didn't just hurt those victims; you destroyed them and their families. You have no idea the pain you have caused so many people."

At that moment, sirens could be heard from a distance. Tran was not aware that Kristy went to the police that morning. They were coming to the crime scene, not aware that he was in the warehouse.

When Tran heard the sirens, he panicked and took out the handgun. He started waving it around, then pointing it at Talina.

"What are you doing? Why are you pointing that at me?" Talina questioned.

"Did you call them? I don't know. I don't know what to do. It's not supposed to happen this way. You have no idea what it's been like for me. I have been tormented everyday with thoughts of wanting to hurt women. I hated women until I met you. You changed everything. I'm not consumed everyday with that anger. I even saw a different future for myself...with you," Tran pleaded, with tears rolling down his face.

Talina backed up a couple feet, dropped to the floor and burst into tears, sobbing, her body racked with grief.

Tran wanted to comfort her, but he was afraid that she would resist him. He also knew the police were getting closer and would be in the warehouse any minute.

"Talina, look at me. Look at me!" Tran demanded as he feared that she would never be able to look at him again. "I'm sorry. I'm sorry Talina." Tran cried out as he knelt down and put his left hand on her right shoulder, while lowering the gun in his right hand.

Abruptly she jumped at his touch. As she looked up, he could see the hurt in her face. Tran stood back up. He started feeling the pain he was putting her through. Panic took hold of the inside of him. "Talina, you have got to understand. I never wanted to hurt you," Tran said as he started to back away from her.

Then, she began to think about her friend, Jasmine. What really happened to her friend, Jasmine? She stood up and started yelling at him. "How could you kill my best friend, Jasmine? I can understand you doing it to strangers, but you knew her, you knew she was my best friend. I don't know if I can ever forgive you for that. Then you moved in to take her place. You didn't stop there. No, you had to create this stalker," she revealed.

Tran's eyes dilated to black. He had no idea she knew about that. This piece of news shattered him.

She finally knew what he was capable of. Talina slowly shook her head back and forth, "How could you? How could you!" Talina shouted over and over as her face reddened with anger. Her emotions went rampant.

Tran shoved the gun in his front right pocket and grabbed her, shaking her shoulders, yelling "Stop it! Stop it!" He couldn't handle the anger that was roaring out of her. Before he knew it, his hands were around her throat. Talina was small and petite. It didn't take much to gain control over her. She started gasping for air, trying desperately to say his name, "Tran. Tran, stop." Her voice lowered to a hoarse whisper. The sadness in her eyes captivated him.

All at once, Tran let go. He realized he was hurting the one person he really cared about. He loved her so much. "I'm sorry Talina. I am so sorry. Please, please forgive me. I don't want you to hate me. I couldn't handle that. You mean more to me than anyone in this world. But I'm never going to have a future with you, am I? I'm never going be able to grow old with you and have a family," he said with sadness.

Suddenly, he looked at her in a calm manner.

He took several steps back, took the gun back out of his pocket and raised the gun to his right temple. His eyes were locked on Talina.

Her eyes widened, "No, don't Tran. Please don't."

With the sounds of police entering the building, Tran was running out of options. They would never take him alive. He knew the end was here. "I love you Talina, but I don't want to hurt you anymore," Tran stated softly as he pulled the trigger. A lone gunshot rang out. His body slowly hit the floor. Blood spewed out everywhere, covering the floor around him.

Talina screamed, as shock set in. It was done. No more women had to die. No more families had to lose their loved ones. The man known as the Cat Scratch Killer lay lifeless at the foot of the only woman he ever loved. He had made his last kill. Trandon would never kill again.

CPSIA information can be obtained
at www.ICGtesting.com
Printed in the USA
FSHW011223031218